Aliens Attack Alpena

Here's what readers from around the country are saying about Johnathan Rand's *AMERICAN CHILLERS:*

" I read THE MICHIGAN MEGA-MONSTERS in one day!" Johnathan Rand's books are AWESOME!
-*Ray M., age 11, Michigan*

"When I read FLORIDA FOG PHANTOMS, it really creeped me out! What a great story!"
-*Carmen T., age 11, Washington, D.C.*

"Johnathan Rand's books are my favorite. They're really creepy and scary!"
-*Jeremy J., age 9, Illinois*

"My whole class loves your books! I have two of them and they are really, really cool."
-*Katie R., age 12, California*

"I never liked to read before, but now I read all the time! The 'Chillers' series is great!"
-*Lauren B., age 10, Ohio*

"I love AMERICAN CHILLERS because they are scary, but not too scary, because I don't want to have nightmares."
-*Adrian P., age 11, Maine*

"I loved it when Johnathan Rand came to our school. He was really funny. His books are great."
-*Jennifer W., age 8, Michigan*

"I read all of the books in the MICHIGAN CHILLERS series and I just started the AMERICAN CHILLERS series. I really love these books!"
-Andrew K., age 13 Montana

"I have six CHILLERS books, and I have read them all three times! I hope I get more for my birthday. My sister loves them, too."
-Jaquann D., age 10, Illinois

"I just read KREEPY KLOWNS OF KALAMAZOO and it really freaked me out a lot. It was really cool!"
-Devin W., age 8, Texas

"THE MICHIGAN MEGA-MONSTERS was great! I hope you write lots more books!"
-Megan P., age 12, Kentucky

"All of my friends love your books! Will you write a book and put my name in it?"
-Michael L., age 10, Ohio

"These books are the best in the world!"
-Garrett M., age 9, Colorado

"We read your books every night. They are really scary and some of them are funny, too."
-Michael & Kristen K., Michigan

"I read THE MICHIGAN MEGA-MONSTERS in two days, and it was cool! When are you going to write one about Wisconsin?"
-John G., age 12, Wisconsin

"Johnathan Rand is my favorite author!"
-*Kelly S., age 8, Michigan*

"AMERICAN CHILLERS are great. I got one
for Christmas, and I loved it. Now, my sister
is reading it. When she's done, I'm going to
read it again."
-*Joel F., age 13, New York*

"I like the CHILLERS books because they are
fun to read. They are scary, too."
-*Hannah K., age 11, Minnesota*

"I read the MEGA-MONSTERS book and I
really liked it. Mr. Rand is a great writer."
-*Ryan M., age 12, Arizona*

"I LOVE AMERICAN CHILLERS!"
-*Zachary R., age 8, Indiana*

"I read your book to my little sister and
she got freaked out. I did, too!"
-*Jason J., age 12, Ohio*

"These books are my favorite! I love reading them!"
-*Sarah N., age 10, New Jersey*

"Your books are great. Please write more so I can read
them.
-*Dylan H., age 7, Tennessee*

Don't miss these exciting, action-packed books by Johnathan Rand:

Michigan Chillers®:

American Chillers®:

Adventure Club series:

www.americanchillers.com

AudioCraft Publishing, Inc.
PO Box 281
Topinabee Island, MI 49791

Johnathan Rand's
MICHIGAN CHILLERS

#4: Aliens Attack Alpena

An AudioCraft Publishing, Inc. book

No part of this publication may be reproduced in whole or in part, or stored in a retrieval system, or transmitted in any form or by any means, electronic, mechanic, photocopying, recording, or otherwise, without written permission from the publisher. For information regarding permission, write to: AudioCraft Publishing, Inc., PO Box 281, Topinabee Island, MI 49791

Michigan Chillers #4: Aliens Attack Alpena
ISBN 1-893699-09-9

Librarians/media specialists:
PCIP/MARC records available at www.americanchillers.com

Cover Illustrations by Dwayne Harris
Cover layout and design by Sue Harring

Printed in USA

ALIENS ATTACK ALPENA

VISIT THE OFFICIAL WORLD HEADQUARTERS OF AMERICAN CHILLERS & MICHIGAN CHILLERS!

The all-new HOME for books by Johnathan Rand! Featuring books, hats, shirts, bookmarks and other cool stuff not available anywhere else in the world! Plus, watch the American Chillers website for news of special events and signings at *CHILLERMANIA* with author Johnathan Rand! Located in northern lower Michigan, on I-75 just off exit 313!

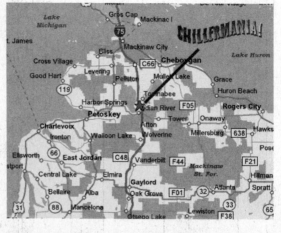

OPENING OCTOBER, 2005!

www.americanchillers.com

1

Boring.

That's how you can describe my life. B-O-R-I-N-G. Nothing exciting ever happens to me. *Nothing.* Well, once I found a twenty-dollar bill while swimming in Hubbard Lake. That was exciting, I guess. But on the level, I think I lead the most boring life in the world.

Little did I know that was all about to change.

It was Monday morning. Another *boring* Monday morning, I might add. First, I have to ride the school bus. Today, of all people, Greg Daniels sat behind me when he got on the bus.

He's a wrestler. Which, I guess, isn't so bad, but Greg likes to pick on people.

Especially *me*.

All the kids on the bus were talking about the meteorite that was sighted in the sky over Alpena last night. I didn't see it, but Dad said that he did. He said that it was a bright ball of fire that swooped overhead. He said it looked like it landed in Lake Huron. That's one of Michigan's Great Lakes. Alpena is a city right next to it. That's where I live.

I was talking to my friend Zack about the meteor. Zack is my age and we have a few classes together.

"Man, that meteorite was really cool!" he said.

"Did you see it?" I asked.

"Yeah!" Zack answered, bobbing his head. "It was awesome! It was a big streak that soared across the sky." As he spoke, he swung his arm from left to right, imitating a streaking, falling star.

See? I miss all the good stuff.

Boring. That's my life.

Suddenly, I felt a hard smack against the side of my head. It hurt! I didn't have to look—I already knew who it was.

Greg Daniels.

He had whacked me up side the head with the palm of his hand. He does that just to annoy people. He likes annoying people . . . and messing up their hair.

"Cut it out!" I said, turning my head as I spoke.

"Oh, and what are *you* going to do about it, twerp?" he sneered, his dark eyes glaring back at me. His hand snapped up and he smacked me again, this time even harder. "Come on," he challenged. "Wanna fight?"

See what I mean? He's nothing but a troublemaker.

"No," I answered sharply, turning back around to face the front of the bus. But I knew it wasn't over.

"I know you won't fight me, because you're a chicken. Bock, bock-bock, bock, bock," he cackled. He sounded just like a chicken! "You're just chicken and you know it,

Blackburn," he finished.

That's my last name. Blackburn. Mark Blackburn. But Greg hardly ever calls anyone by their first name. He usually uses their last name. Not only is he a bully . . . but he's a *rude* bully. Greg is thirteen. I'm twelve, but I'll be thirteen in two weeks. Hooray! A teenager. I can't wait.

Of course, if I get into a fight with Greg Daniels, I might not *live* to see my thirteenth birthday! Greg is a lot bigger . . . and stronger than I am.

I did *not* want to get into a fight with Greg Daniels.

But, as luck would have it, it looked like a fight was going to be unavoidable. Here's what happened:

Greg always gets off the bus first. He usually jumps out of his seat and pushes other kids out of his way so he can be the first off the bus.

When we got to school, Greg leapt up even before the bus had stopped.

"See ya later, chicken," he said to me as he

stood up. As soon as he stepped out into the aisle and started forward, he stumbled . . . and fell flat on his face!

Everyone on the bus laughed at him. Even me! It *was* pretty funny. I think he got what he deserved.

But it looked like I was about to get what I *didn't* deserve!

Greg had tripped over my backpack! He didn't see it on the floor, and he tumbled, falling forward and landing smack dab in the middle of the aisle.

The other kids on the bus were still laughing as he stood up and turned around. He looked down and saw my olive-green backpack.

Then he looked at me.

He was *mad!* His dark eyebrows were scrunched together, and his forehead was wrinkled. His hair was messed up and his face was as red as a tomato. His nostrils flared. He was really embarrassed.

"You're going to pay for this one, chicken," he said bitingly, clenching his teeth together.

He stepped closer, leaning toward me. "Get

ready to get creamed, chicken. Your luck has just run out."

I closed my eyes, waiting for the worst.

2

"Greg, knock it off," the bus driver suddenly boomed. Greg turned around and saw the bus driver looking at him, then turned back to me.

"*You're going to pay for this, chicken,*" he said in a quieter voice that still trembled with fury. "*Wait till I see you on the bus tonight. You'll pay for this.*"

Great. I might as well just make out my will right now. I'm going to die. Looks like I won't live to see my thirteenth birthday, after all.

Well, at least my short life wasn't so boring anymore.

All day long, I did nothing but worry about the bus trip home. I couldn't even pay attention

17

in class. In my history class, we had a movie about the American revolution. Then we had a quiz afterwards, and I missed almost every question.

In my English class, I sit next to Carly Gordon. I have to admit, I really have a crush on her. She has long, blonde hair and she's very pretty.

But I was so wigged-out about the bus ride home that I couldn't even *think* about her!

In science class, all we did was talk about the meteorite. My teacher explained that meteors are pieces of space rock that fly through space very fast. Once in a while, they enter the earth's atmosphere. Most of them burn up before they hit the earth's surface, but a few of them don't.

Like the one last night. On the news, they said the meteorite had crashed into Lake Huron. I was really interested, but I was too worried about getting decked by Greg Daniels.

Then, in my last class, I had an idea. Actually, the idea was given to me by my friend, Meghan. I've known her ever since the first grade. She's one of my best friends. Meghan has short brown hair and she's the exact same height as I am.

She leaned over to talk to me when the teacher wasn't looking.

"I heard you're going to fight Greg Daniels on the bus," she whispered.

Great. I think the whole school knew I was going to get creamed. Maybe somebody should sell tickets.

"Well, I sure don't want to," I whispered back.

"What did you do to make him so mad at you?" she asked. Her eyes were wide. I'm sure she knew that there was no way I could win a fight with Greg Daniels.

When I told her how Greg had tripped over my backpack, she started laughing. "Good!" she hissed. "It's about time he gets a taste of his own medicine."

"The problem is, that medicine is going to be hard for me to swallow on the bus ride home," I said quietly, shaking my head.

We were both silent for a few moments.

Meghan went back to writing something, then she stopped. She turned her head toward me, her eyes all big and round.

"Hey, I've got an idea!" she whispered. "Why don't you just 'miss' the bus? I mean . . . you don't have to ride the bus home."

"I thought about that," I said. And I had. I thought that if I didn't ride the bus home, then I wouldn't have to fight Greg. But how would I get home? I lived ten miles from school. I certainly couldn't walk ten miles!

"You could ride my brother's mountain bike home," Meghan offered. "He won't care. We only live a couple blocks from the school. We can walk there. You can take his bike."

Now *that* was an idea. Ten miles is a long way to go, but if I had a bicycle . . . .

"You really think he wouldn't mind if I borrowed his bike?" I whispered, trying to keep silent so that our teacher wouldn't hear.

"Nah. He's pretty cool. I'm sure it would be okay with him."

Suddenly, my spirits were lifted. Maybe I might live to see my thirteenth birthday, after all.

"Meet me behind the school and we'll walk to my house," Meghan said.

When class was over I had to walk through the hall to my locker. Man, I hoped I didn't run into Greg! He might decide that he wasn't going to wait till I got on the bus.

Thankfully, I didn't see him.

That is, of course, until I went outside . . .

3

He was waiting for me.

Right outside the doors of the school.

"Ready to die, chicken?" he sneered. His hands were doubled into fists, ready for action. A group of other kids started to gather around.

This was it. I was a goner.

Greg took a step forward, and I took a step back.

"What's the matter, chicken?" he mocked. "Bock, bock, bock-bock, bock . . . ."

Soon all of the other kids around were doing the same thing.

"*Bock, bock-bock, bock, bock-bock,*" the group chanted.

I took another step back and bumped into someone. The chanting suddenly stopped, and I spun.

It was the principal, Mr. Greene. Mr. Greene is short and hardly has any hair. He's a nice guy, and most kids like him.

Was I ever glad to see *him!*

"I think that will be just about enough of this horseplay," he said, speaking to the small crowd that had gathered. "Go on. You all have buses to catch."

Saved! Well . . . at least for the time being.

The crowd of kids began to thin out, and I caught a glimpse of Meghan. She was standing by the sidewalk at the end of a line of buses. She nodded her head, indicating for me to sneak away.

Greg Daniels turned and began walking toward the bus. He glanced over his shoulder every few seconds to make sure I was coming.

I had an idea. If I could make Greg just *think* that I was coming, then he would get on the bus!

When he did, I could take off running! There's no way he would be able to do anything!

It was the only chance I had.

I slowly began walking toward the bus. There was a short line of students waiting to get on. Greg was in the back, so I walked slow.

Come on, I thought. *Hurry up and get on the bus. Hurry up . . . .*

It seemed to take forever for him to board the bus. I watched him take a step up, then another, then look back over his shoulder at me. He had this really sick grin on his face. I think he would really enjoy beating me up.

Finally, I was the last one standing at the door of the bus.

"Well?" the bus driver asked. "Are you riding, or aren't you?"

Now!

I turned and ran as fast as I could. My sneakers smacked on the pavement as I bolted along the row of parked buses. I carried my backpack in one hand, swinging it madly back and forth as I sprinted down the sidewalk.

I saw Meghan up ahead of me. She had

been waiting, wondering what I was going to do.

I managed a quick glance behind me, and what I saw sent a wave of terror through my body.

Greg.

He had gotten off the bus somehow, and now he was in hot pursuit! I could hear his footsteps thundering behind me.

This was a nightmare! I didn't think Greg would be able to get off the bus. I thought that once he was on the bus, he'd be stuck.

Could I outrun him?

I had to. I just *had* to.

So much for my boring life!

Fear can make you do funny things, sometimes. Just seeing Greg made me run even faster. I was determined that I would outrun him.

I caught up to Meghan and she started running with me.

"*This way!*" she yelled, pointing toward the forest. "I know a trail! If we can get there, we can lose him in the forest!"

I hoped she was right.

Behind us, Greg seemed to be getting tired. He wasn't running as fast, and we had been able to put some distance between us.

But he was still chasing us, fast and furious. *"I'm going to get you, chicken!"* he shouted. *"You're in for it now!"* He was as mad as ever.

"Over there!" Meghan heaved, as we jumped over branches and brush. I hoped she knew where she was going!

The woods became thicker and thicker. Branches tore at my arms and face, and we couldn't run very fast. Once I almost tripped and fell.

Suddenly, we came to a trail! Meghan was right!

But we could still hear Greg behind us, trudging through the thick forest.

"You just wait, chicken!" he shouted.

"Come on!" Meghan yelled frantically as she started up the path. "We can hide in the woods!"

"Where does this path go?" I managed to ask between heavy gulps of air. I was getting tired of running. The forest was dense and the branches were thick.

"It goes way back into the forest," she answered. "But there are lots of places to hide. Over here!"

Suddenly, she bolted off the trail and went behind a thick clump of small willows. I couldn't see her!

"Where are you?" I asked.

"Shhhh!" she replied in a voice just above a whisper. *"I'm right here!"*

I took a few steps toward the willows and sure enough, she was crouched down low. It was almost impossible to see her! The branches were very thick.

I fell to the ground and rolled sideways next to Meghan. The only thing I could hear was the sound of my own heart beating. And birds. Lots of birds sang from high in the trees.

We waited.

"Do you think we've lost him?" I whispered between heaving breaths.

"I don't know," Meghan answered.

In an instant, we knew. We could hear the

crunching of footsteps along the trail, not far away.

Had he seen us? Did he know we had left the trail?

Suddenly, we heard Greg's voice.

"I know you're out here somewhere," he said, his voice raised in anger.

I shuddered. If he found me now, I would *really* get it!

"Uh-oh," I heard Greg say in a mocking voice. "Hey, chicken . . . *I can seeeeeeeeeeee yoooooouuuuuuuu.*"

Suddenly, I heard breaking branches and the crunching of footsteps.

Greg had found us! He had found our hiding place!

4

All of a sudden, Meghan burst up from the ground and began running . . . *deeper into the swamp!*

I had no choice. I jumped up and ran after her.

Behind us, I could hear Greg lumbering through the branches. Twigs snapped and popped as he took up chase. It was harder going for Greg, since he was so much bigger than Meghan and I.

The forest grew thicker, but Meghan pressed on, pushing limbs out of her way as we trudged through the dense underbrush. We kept going for what seemed like hours.

Finally, Meghan stopped and turned to look behind us. I did the same.

There was no sign of Greg. We stood for a few minutes, listening for any sign of him plowing through the woods, but there was none. The forest was quiet, except for the peaceful chirping of birds.

"Whew," I said, breathing a sigh of relief. "That was close."

Meghan opened her mouth to speak, but she was interrupted by a strange noise in the distance. It sounded like a radio being tuned.

"What on earth is that?" she said.

We listened. The noise became a low hum. But we couldn't see where it was coming from.

"I think it's coming from over there, on the other side of those cedar trees," I said, pointing with my arm.

Meghan turned and led the way, and I followed. The humming grew louder.

We crept up to a line of cedars and crouched down. Whatever was making the noise was just on the other side of the trees.

I thought that it might be a small factory of some sort . . . but I've never heard of a factory in the middle of the woods!

Slowly, very slowly, I crept up and peeked through the branches.

"*Whoaaa!!*" I whispered. I froze. My eyes grew wide and my jaw fell.

"What is it?" Meghan asked, getting to her feet.

There was no way I could explain it. This she would have to see for herself.

Sitting in a small clearing was a spaceship! There was no doubt about it. It was egg-shaped and silver, about the size of a large van. Two antennas protruded out of the top. There were no windows, but there was a door on the side, and a row of blue and green flashing lights that went all around the middle. The lights flashed and chased around the ship like a string of Christmas lights.

Meghan's mouth opened, but no sound came out. Neither of us spoke.

"*It's . . . it's a spaceship,*" she finally

whispered.

I had only *heard* stories about spaceships before. I read somewhere about some spaceship that was supposed to have crashed about fifty years ago, and someone was keeping the remains of the spaceship in their locked garage. I didn't know if it was true or not.

All of a sudden the humming stopped. The flashing lights blinked a few more times and then went out. All was quiet.

Except—

A door was opening! The door of the spaceship began to screech open! Someone—or *something*—was coming out!

5

Meghan and I were too afraid to move. The door of the spaceship was opening, and a row of steps was slowly extending down. Soon, the door was all the way open. Metal steps stretched all the way down to the ground.

We waited. Nothing else happened.

"This can't be real," Meghan whispered.

But there it was, right in front of us—a spaceship.

Where had it come from? Was it some kind of government experiment that we weren't supposed to know about? If so, we could get in a lot of trouble.

But, then again, if it was a *real* spaceship from another planet, we'd *really* be in trouble! Maybe they were weird creatures from Jupiter or something!

Suddenly a noise came from the ship. It was a clanking sound, and it seemed to be coming from inside the spacecraft! Meghan and I stood frozen, peering through the branches. She grabbed my hand and held it tightly. She was scared.

But, I must admit, I was kind of scared myself. It's not every day that you find a spaceship in the woods!

"*Look,*" I whispered. I could see movement in the spaceship.

In the next moment, we saw it. It was a creature of some sort. About my size, or maybe a bit smaller. It looked like it had some type of suit on, but I couldn't be sure. There were too many branches blocking my view.

More noise and shuffling.

Suddenly, the creature came out of the spaceship! He was walking down the steps! We could hear the metal clanging as he climbed down.

Then the noise stopped. Whoever—or whatever—it was, was on the ground.

"Can you see him?" Meghan whispered.

"No," I whispered back. *"There's too much brush in the way."*

Should I take the chance and try and pull some branches away so I could see better? If I did, it might make some noise, and we might be found out. Then what would happen?

But I desperately wanted to see the space alien . . . or whatever it was.

I shifted my feet and slowly leaned forward. I still couldn't see very well.

But I decided to take a chance. I decided I would try and pull some branches back so that Meghan and I could see better.

"What are you doing?!" Meghan whispered, her voice tense with fear. I didn't answer. Instead, I slowly reached forward and used my arm to sweep some of the branches from our view.

Now I could see clearly—and what I saw

made me just about jump right out of my skin!

6

A space creature. There was no doubt about it.

Actually, we really couldn't see the creature very well, because he had a space suit on. It was a silvery suit that looked a lot like tin foil. He had a helmet and a dark shield that covered his face.

And he was carrying a gun!

At least, it sure looked like a gun. It looked like something from *Star Wars* or *Battlestar Galactica*.

I could feel Meghan's hand tighten over mine. She was really scared now.

As we watched, the creature began walking

around the outside of the spaceship. It looked like he was checking for damage or something.

He continued on his way, walking around the entire spacecraft. Finally, he stopped at the bottom of the stairs. He took one final look around the area, and I froze when he looked in our direction.

Could he see us? Maybe he had super-vision, like an eagle or something.

Seconds passed, and finally, the alien turned away.

That was a close one.

But it wasn't over quite yet. Just as the creature was taking a step back up into the spacecraft, Meghan sneezed.

"Ahhhh . . . CHOOOOO!"

The alien stopped and spun back around, facing us. His gun was aimed right at us!

We were goners for sure! I could see the headlines in the newspaper the next day. *Nosy Kids Killed by Space Alien*, the headline would read.

"I'm sorry," Meghan whispered, her voice trembling. *"I couldn't hold it any longer."*

We stood there, hoping that the space alien hadn't seen us. Maybe—just maybe—his vision was very bad, and he couldn't see well at all.

Without warning, his face shield rotated up, exposing his face. He had two huge, glossy-black eyes that were the size of baseballs. His nose was flat, and his mouth was a lot like a human's mouth, only the creature didn't appear to have any lips!

But I knew that he was looking at us.

I *knew* we had been spotted.

We had to do something. This was dangerous. I had no idea what a space alien might do. Especially a space alien with a gun!

It was a stand-off. We stood staring at each other, none of us moving. We just waited. We waited and we watched each other.

The creature moved first. He slowly lowered his gun and aimed it at the ground.

It was the chance we needed.

"Run!" I shouted, pulling Meghan back from the line of brush. "Run as fast as you can!"

Still holding my hand, Meghan turned and we ran . . . or tried to. The branches were too thick, and when I took my first step, I tripped . . . .

And fell.

Man, if anything could go wrong today, it was going to! First Greg on the bus, now a space alien in the woods! In fact, if it hadn't been for Greg, we wouldn't be in the mess we were in!

I jumped back up to my feet, but I couldn't resist just taking one last look at the space creature.

What I saw horrified me!

The alien had his gun to his shoulder, and he was aiming it right at me!

That was the last thing I remembered. It was the last thing I remembered because the alien opened fire.

He had shot me with his laser gun.

7

The next thing I knew, everything was yellow. I couldn't see anything. Trees, sky, Meghan—nothing. It was like I was surrounded by a brilliant yellow light.

What was going on? What had happened? I had been trying to run from the space alien, and he had shot me.

Was I dead? Where was Meghan? Where was the space alien?

Then things around me began to clear. I could make out trees and the ground. And Meghan. She was standing right next to me.

But we seemed to be in some weird ball. There was a yellow wall all around us.

"What . . . what happened?" she said quietly, with more than a hint of fear in her voice.

"I think we got shot by a laser gun," I answered.

"I thought space aliens only had laser guns in the movies," Meghan said.

Suddenly, we heard a crunching noise.

Footsteps.

The space alien! He was coming toward us!

Again, we tried to run . . . and ran right smack into the strange glowing wall around us.

We were trapped!

The creature came closer and closer, and stopped just a few feet from the glowing yellow ball that was holding us captive. He had the laser gun aimed at us.

Suddenly the yellow ball disappeared! It faded away in just a few seconds. We were left standing in the forest with a space alien just a few feet away.

And he didn't look happy.

"QIOQJIBLILIBDAYNJDB!!" he said.

Huh? What in the world was that? It just sounded like jibberish. I had never heard of a language like that before.

Of course, I had never seen a space alien before, either. It would only make sense that they would have their own language.

"QIOQJIBLILIBDAYNJDB!" the creature demanded again, only louder this time.

"I . . . I don't know what you mean," I answered. But if I didn't know what *he* meant, how was he going to know what *I* meant?

The alien looked puzzled. He squinted his huge, bug-like eyes and twitched his nose. His mouth was open just a crack, but no sound came out.

Then he did a strange thing.

On the front of his space suit was a small door. It wasn't a pocket, but an actual door that opened just like you would expect a door to open. Still leveling the laser gun at us, he carefully opened up the door with his free hand. I saw some blinking lights and some switches and dials.

He made a few adjustments, and began to speak.

"JLOAUJKS," he said. "SKJDHIU . . . TESJHSKJD . . . TEST, KJXTYS . . . TESTDJH . . . TESTIN . . . JHYTLTING . . . TESTING, 1, 2, 3, HJGHXSKJD . . .TESTING, 1, 2, 3, 4 . . . Ah. There we go."

English! The creature could speak English!

He closed the small door on his suit and looked back up at us.

"Now . . . tell me who you are," the space alien demanded. His voice sounded almost like a robot. It was raspy and maybe a bit hoarse, like he had a cold or a stuffy nose. I figured that he must have some kind of built-in computer that would allow him to change languages.

Man, I wish I had one of those! That would be cool!

"Ummm," I began. "I'm Mark Blackburn. This is Meghan Andrews."

The space alien showed no expression.

"What planet are you from?" he asked.

"Well, uh . . . *this* one. This planet, right here. Earth."

Hearing this, the creature seemed to ease. He lowered the gun.

"Ah yes," he said. "Earthlings. I was told to expect you. My, you are strange looking creatures."

Hey! Who was he calling strange?!?!? *He* was the strange one!! He looked like a giant bug wrapped in foil!

"What do you want with us?" Meghan managed to ask.

Good question.

"Nothing," the alien replied. "I am here to destroy the Globblings."

The what?!?!? I thought. *What in the world are Globblings?*

I really wanted to know. So I asked him.

"The Globblings? What's a Globbling?"

"The Globblings are from the planet Globbla," the alien said. "Awful creatures, they are. They are here to take over your planet."

"Take over the planet?!?!?" Meghan stammered, her eyes bugging out of her head. *"Aliens from outer space?!?!"*

"Actually, they are aliens from *inner* space,"

the creature answered.

Say what? *Inner* space? What was he talking about?

"They came to your planet a short time ago. The Globblings are very small, but they grow very large very quickly."

"Well, where are they?" I asked.

"They need deep water," the alien said. "That is what is called 'inner' space. That is where they begin. The Globblings feed on underwater creatures until they grow big enough to leave the water."

"Then what do they eat?" I asked.

"Why, earthlings, of course," the alien said. "They are here to take over the entire planet by eating all the people of earth. That's what Globblings do."

Oh no!

8

I thought about the events of the day, and how Greg Daniels had threatened to beat me up. I thought about how scared I had been, and how scared I was when he was chasing me.

But that was nothing.

Now I was *really* scared.

"But . . . how? Why?" I asked. A hundred questions spun through my head.

"The Globblings start out very small." To show us, the alien took off his glove, exposing a strange, three-fingered hand. His skin was brown and looked like it might have had scales.

I thought that maybe he was like some kind of lizard or something.

He reached his hand up and made a small circle with his fingers. The circle was about the size of a quarter.

"That's how big they are?" Meghan asked, almost laughing. The space alien nodded.

"But they grow very quickly," the creature said. "They travel in a single spaceship. The spaceship goes directly into the water, as deep as possible. That's why no one sees them until it's too late. Once they reach land . . . there may be no stopping them."

This was too much. Aliens from space? Attacking Alpena?

Crazy.

"Their spaceship landed here last night. They're somewhere close by, under water. I have been sent here to destroy them."

My eyes suddenly lit up.

"Lake Huron!" I exclaimed, remembering the meteorite that had been spotted in the sky last night. "That wasn't a meteorite, after all! I'll bet their spaceship crashed into Lake Huron!

It's very deep . . . and no one would know that they are there!"

"What do they look like?" Meghan asked.

The space alien thought for a moment.

"When they're small, they don't look like much of anything," he replied. "Just blobs of red jelly. As they grow, they begin to take shape. After they grow, the Globblings look like a cross between a human and a lizard, except they have wings, and they are very strong and powerful. The more they eat, the bigger and stronger they get. They are hideous creatures, really."

I couldn't believe what I was hearing. I couldn't believe what I was *seeing,* either. I was talking to a real live space alien . . . and he was telling me that he was here to destroy *other* space aliens . . . space aliens that were here to destroy the world!

"Please," the creature said. "You must show me where this 'Lake Huron' is. That is where I must look."

"It's not hard to find," Meghan said. "Lake Huron is huge."

"Take me there. We must hurry." The creature began walking back to his spacecraft. When he realized we weren't following him, he stopped and turned around.

"Please. We must hurry."

"What?" I asked, my mouth hanging open like a dead fish. "You want us to go with you? In *that?!??!*" I nodded toward the spaceship.

"Yes, of course," he said. "You don't have these here on earth?" He pointed to his spacecraft.

"Well, no," I said. "We have cars. They're a bit smaller and they stay on the ground. We have planes, too, and helicopters. But they don't look anything like the thing you've got."

The creature looked very puzzled with this.

"No matter," he said. "But come. We must find where the Globblings are hiding."

I looked at Meghan. Meghan looked at me, then we looked at the strange creature.

"We're not supposed to ride with strangers," Meghan said.

"Oh, silly me," the space alien replied. He walked back toward us and extended his three-fingered hand. I slowly clasped it. His hand felt warm and stiff.

"Brothron is my name," he said. I am from the planet Vargondan. I am known as a Vargon."

"Nice to meet you, Brothron," I said.

"The pleasure is mine." He turned and introduced himself to Meghan, and she reluctantly took his hand.

"There," he said. "Now we're not strangers. Now we can go aboard my spaceship." He turned and began walking toward the craft.

I followed.

So did Meghan.

We were about to take a ride on a real spaceship. I didn't know it at the time, but it was about to become the most important ride of my life.

9

I held my breath as I climbed the steps . . . the steps that led into the spacecraft. Meghan was right behind me.

The inside of the ship didn't look much different than an airplane cockpit. There were lots of dials and levers, and a big windshield in the front. Four chairs were fastened to the floor in front of a huge control panel.

"Make sure you buckle yourselves in tight," Brothron said.

Meghan and I each sat in a chair and strapped ourselves in. The strap was a lot like a seat belt in a car . . . it came up over my shoulder and fastened at the waist.

"This thing really flies?" Meghan asked.

"Yes, this is one of the newer models. I've got to get it back to have it looked at, though. I think something is wrong with the throttle. I can only go about three hundred thousand miles an hour."

Three hundred thousand miles an hour?!?!? I thought. *Is he kidding?*

No, he probably wasn't. After all . . . he was from a different planet. Why would he kid me about how fast his spacecraft flew?

We heard a noise behind us as the door closed. Then the inside of the ship went dark.

Suddenly, engines roared to life. Lights began to blink and flicker, and the drone of the craft was deafening.

The craft began to rise straight up in the air! It was a weird feeling. I've never been in a helicopter before, but I imagined that this would be what it would feel like. Within seconds, we were high above the trees.

"Over there," I said, pointing to the vast blue sea that was coming into view. "That's

Lake Huron."

"I expected as much when I flew over the first time," Brothron said. "But I needed to land on the ground to determine if the Globblings have already invaded or not."

"Invaded?" I asked. "Already? You mean . . . they can attack *that* fast?"

"Oh yes. I know that they're planning this very minute. They will stop at nothing to wipe out the earth. That is why we must hurry before it's too late. We must hurry and destroy them while they are small. If they grow too large, we will never stop them."

The spacecraft began to lurch forward, and I could feel us moving faster and faster. The ground below us was a blur, but I could make out my school, and buildings downtown. I saw Thunder Bay Shores marina, and even a bunch of boats in the water.

We were *really* moving fast, now. I could hear the hum of the spacecraft growing louder and louder.

Below us, the land gave way to Lake Huron. The sun glistened on the glimmering surface.

Soon, there was nothing below us but crystal-blue water.

Suddenly the spaceship shook violently and plummeted toward the water!

Meghan let out a scream, and so did I. The only thing we could see through the windshield was the surface of Lake Huron—and we were headed right for it!

We were going down! The spaceship was crashing!

10

I didn't have time to scream again. The only thing I could do was hold my breath and close my eyes.

Crash! The impact of the craft hitting the water threw me forward, but my seatbelt caught me. I waited for water to rush in, and wondered how I would get out of the doomed craft.

The water never came.

I opened my eyes. We were underwater! It was incredible, but the spacecraft survived the impact! The surrounding waters were a greenish-blue.

In the seat next to me, Meghan had covered

her face with her hands. After a moment, she pulled them away. Her mouth was open, and her eyes were wide.

"Where . . . where are we?" she asked softly.

"Why, we're in Lake Huron," Brothron said, very matter-of-factly.

I could tell we were going deeper, because everything was getting darker. The windshield in front of us faded from dark blue to almost pitch black.

"Looks like we'll need some light," Brothron said, and he reached forward and flicked a switch.

Suddenly, bright lights illuminated the water! We could see! It was really cool, being able to see under the water like that. It was like being in a submarine!

"Look!" Meghan said, pointing.

A huge fish came into view, and Brothron swerved the craft to go around it. It was a big fish, too . . . almost as big as the one my Dad said he *almost* caught last summer.

"We'll have to go slower in the water," Brothron said. "And we also have to be careful.

If the Globblings see the lights from the spacecraft, we'll be in trouble."

"What are we looking for?" I asked. I mean . . . I had no clue what to look for. All I knew was that the invading aliens were supposed to be small, red blobs . . . until they eat. Then they got bigger.

"Well, I'm not even sure myself," Brothron answered. "But I'm sure that they will stay close to their spacecraft . . . at least until they grow larger."

My curiosity was killing me. I had to know.

"Just how big can these Globblings get?" I asked.

"As big as they want," Brothron replied. "They never stop growing. The more they eat, the bigger they get. Why, I've seen Globblings the size of your planet."

As big as our planet?!?!? I thought. If I ever had a choice between fighting a Globbling and fighting Greg Daniels, I think I would choose Greg Daniels! This morning it might have been a different story, but now . . . .

"If Globblings get that big, just how are we

going to destroy them?" Meghan asked. I wanted to know, too. It sounded like a pretty big job.

"It's quite simple, really," Brothron said. "We just blast them with high-intensity photron lasers. It's the only way of getting rid of unsightly Globblings."

Huh? High intense *what?* I thought that only Luke Skywalker or Han Solo from *Star Wars* had those. I guess photron lasers were real, after all.

"How do you use them?" I asked. "Are they like the one you shot at us?"

"Oh no, not at all," Brothron said, shaking his head. "Yes, it was a photron laser . . . but I had it set for 'freeze'. It didn't hurt you . . . it just kept you from getting away. This spaceship has two photron laser guns . . . they're both set at the highest level."

"Yeah, but how do they work?" Meghan asked.

"You'll find out in a second," Brothron said, leaning closer to the control panel. "I think I see a Globbling right now."

Meghan and I strained our eyes to see in the murky depths. Even with the bright lights on, the waters beneath the surface of Lake Huron were very, very dark.

Suddenly, we saw it.

A Globbling.

And everything that Brothron said about them was right.

It was a red, jelly-like blob, about the size of a beach ball. It just sort of floated in the water in front of the spacecraft. But when I looked closer, I could see eyes. I could see eyes, a nose, and a mouth.

It was gross!

It was like a ball of jelly floating around in the water.

Only much, much worse. I could see what Brothron was talking about. It looked like the creature was growing arms, legs, and wings.

And it looked mean. Its face was twisted in anger, and its mouth was open. It looked like something out of one of my comic books.

When the spaceship got closer to the alien, the blob began to change. I could see sharp teeth begin to form in its mouth. Something told me that these Globblings were not something to mess with.

Suddenly, Brothron reached out and pressed a button on the panel. A brilliant yellow beam streaked through the water. It struck the blob, and there was a bright flash, and a thundering blast shook the entire spaceship.

The blob exploded! The light from the explosion was so bright that I had to close my eyes. Meghan did, too.

"Wow," I said.

"Double-wow," Meghan said.

"What does 'wow' mean?" Brothron asked.

"Well, it's just an expression," I answered. "It means that we're impressed."

Brothron smiled. It was the first time I had seen him smile.

"Well, it's an ugly job, but somebody's got to do it," he said.

I guess I thought that if all we had to do was go through the water and shoot Globblings, this whole thing would be pretty easy.

Man . . . I didn't know how wrong I was—but I was about to find out!

12

I've never been in a submarine before, and I've never been below the surface more than a few feet. But now here we were, hundreds of feet below the surface of Lake Huron! It was eerie. The engine of the spacecraft hummed quietly, and the waters around us were dark, except where the beam of light was. It was like being in a dark, misty cave.

"They must be around here somewhere," Brothron said, his bug-like eyes searching the dark waters before us.

"Right there!" Meghan suddenly cried. "What's *that?!?!?*"

She pointed, but I couldn't see anything.

Then a blob came into view.

It was red. And it was big.

"Uh-oh," Brothron said quietly. "They're growing fast. They're much larger than I thought."

The red blob in front of us was about the size of me. In the bright lights, it looked soft and jelly-like. It was very strange looking, indeed. I mean . . . it looked just like a blob of jelly drifting through the dark water.

Weird.

But as we drew closer, I saw something else. I saw its eyes and its mouth. And arms and legs. And wings sprouting from the back of the blob.

"They're growing quickly," Brothron said. "It won't be long before they leave the water and begin their attack on land."

My skin crawled. It was hard to imagine that weird blob growing into one of those creepy creatures.

Without another word, Brothron reached forward. He grasped a lever and made some adjustments, all the while watching the huge blob in front of us.

All at once there was a flash as a thin beam of light shot out from beneath the spacecraft! The beam rocketed through the murky depths and hit the blob, and once again, a booming thunder rocked the ship. In the next instant, the only thing left of the Globbling were tiny shreds of red, gooey pieces. They swirled about harmlessly in the dark waters.

"You got him!" I exclaimed. I wished that I could have one of those laser blasters for Greg Daniels.

Well, not really. I didn't want to *hurt* Greg.

But if I had a laser blaster like Brothron's, Greg Daniels sure wouldn't bother me anymore!

"How many more Globblings are there?" Meghan asked.

"There might be ten, there might be a hundred," Brothron answered. He shrugged. "There's no telling how many there might be."

A hundred?!?!?! We'd never be able to find and stop a hundred Globblings! If what Brothron said was right, they were growing too fast!

"WATCH OUT!" Meghan suddenly screamed, her arm upraised and pointing.

But it was too late. The spaceship was moving too fast in the water—and there was a Globbling right in front of us.

We were going to hit!

13

Brothron tried to turn the ship and veer out of the way, but it was no use. Even *he* knew we were going to hit.

"Hold on!" Brothron shouted. I grabbed the edges of my seat, and Meghan did the same.

We hit. The impact pushed me forward in the seat, and I could hear the spaceship's motor stall.

Suddenly, the entire windshield was covered with red jelly. The huge Globbling looked as if it had spread itself out over the entire spacecraft. We lurched to one side, then the other.

Then we began to fall! The spaceship lost power, and we began to tumble into the depths. All of the lights blinked off, and a warning siren began to sound.

"What's happening?!?!?" I shouted.

"The Globbling has diffused our energy source!" Brothron said. "We need to use the emergency power generator!"

The spacecraft was dark, and tumbling wildly in the depths. I could feel us falling farther and farther, down to the deepest part of Lake Huron.

Meghan wasn't saying anything. I think she was too afraid.

I could hear Brothron shuffling around in the darkness.

"Come on, come on," he said, speaking to no one in particular. I could hear switches click on and off. I knew he was trying to get the emergency power supply to start up.

Suddenly, lights blinked on in the ship! The engines began to hum, and whir!

We had power!

Brothron leapt back into his seat. The huge,

red Globbling still covered the windshield before us. It was all we could see.

"Well, now it's time to take care of *you*," he said, staring at the Globbling through the thick glass.

"One . . . two . . . ."

He paused for only an instant.

" — Three," he finished. Brothron flicked a switch.

There was a terrible scream from outside the craft! The Globbling released its hold and drifted back from the spaceship.

"What did you do?" I asked.

"I just sent an electric charge to the outside of the spacecraft," Brothron answered. "That Globbling just got the shock of his life."

Once again, I thought about how strange this day had been. This morning, I was on a school bus, being threatened by that bully, Greg Daniels. Now I was at the bottom of Lake Huron, hunting down Globblings . . . with an alien from another planet!

I felt the spacecraft move backwards, and the Globbling began to drift off.

"He's getting away!" I cried.

"Oh, no he's not," Brothron said. He fired a laser and the creature exploded! He blew up just like the first two!

"All right!" I shouted, throwing my fist into the air. I had to admit, this was kind of exciting. It's not every day you get to hunt down space aliens!

The spacecraft started moving again, and it wasn't long before we spotted another Globbling. It was about the same size as the other two, but it looked . . . well . . . *different.*

"Uh-oh," Brothron said quietly. The spaceship stopped, and it was then that I noticed the Globbling was moving. He was gliding away from us.

"What's wrong?" Meghan asked.

"They're growing fast, Brothron replied. "Look closely at that one."

The spaceship followed behind the Globbling at a safe distance. I looked closer, and it was then that I knew what Brothron was talking about.

The Globbling had grown wings! He had

wings, and legs and arms. And a tail. Up until now, most of the Globblings we had seen weren't fully grown. This one was. It was really ugly looking.

"He's trying to get to the surface," Brothron said, his robot-like voice filled with concern.

And he was right.

We followed the creature through the water as it rose upward. It swam through the water expertly, gliding up through the murky blue. Just as it reached the surface, Brothron fired. The laser shot through the water like lightning, and, for the fourth time that day, a Globbling exploded into a million tiny, blood-red shreds.

"We're too late," Brothron said solemnly.

"What do you mean?" I asked, fearing the worst.

"The Globblings," Brothron began, "are leaving the water. They are growing in size much faster than I thought. I'm afraid they've begun to attack the city."

Oh my gosh! Aliens were attacking Alpena!

14

The spaceship exploded out of the water, and we were in the air again.

"We must hurry!" Brothron said.

I hadn't a clue what he meant.

In the distance, I could see the city of Alpena. I wondered if anyone knew of the danger they were about to face.

"There's one right there," Brothron said, pointing his three-fingered hand down to the waters below us. Sure enough, a red blob was emerging from the water.

Brothron turned the ship and we headed down. He aimed the photron laser and fired.

The beam of light shot from the craft and sliced through the water next to the Globbling.

"Missed," Brothron said. He turned the ship once again, and fired another shot.

Bullseye! The Globbling exploded, and traces of red, slimy goo was the only thing left.

"Good shot!" Meghan said.

Brothron pulled the spaceship control lever back, and we headed high into the sky. Once again, we could see the buildings and streets of Alpena. As we drew closer, we could see cars and trucks, and even people walking about.

But thankfully, no Globblings.

Not yet, anyway.

Brothron steered the ship to a wooded area on the outskirts of town. There were no houses around, and the craft landed gently in a small field. The door opened, and the steps rolled out.

"Now, the *real* work begins," Brothron said.

He unbuckled his seat belt and got out of his seat. Meghan and I did the same.

"Remember . . . this is going to be dangerous. Globblings are nasty creatures. They will eat almost anything . . . or anyone.

Here . . . take these."

Brothron reached into his belt and pulled out two small guns. At least, they looked like guns. But they were blue and yellow and had a very wide barrel.

"What are those?" I asked.

"Photron lasers," he continued, and he handed one to Meghan and one to me. "They look small, but they are very powerful. They have different settings."

He showed us how to use the settings, explaining that there was a 'low' power and a 'high' power.

"You'll use the high power to kill the Globblings," Brothron instructed. "The low power won't do anything but freeze them."

"Kind of like when you blasted us earlier?" Meghan asked.

"Exactly," Brothron answered. "Now . . . you must hurry." He sat back down in his seat.

"What . . . what are you doing?" I stammered.

"We have to split up. I am going to go back into the lake to search for more Globblings . . .

and the mother ship."

"You're leaving us?!?!?" Meghan cried. "You're leaving us to fight the Globblings?!?!? All by ourselves?!?!?"

"I'm afraid there is no other way," Brothron answered. "Hurry! When you find a Globbling, use your photron lasers. Hurry, while there's still time to save the planet!"

We ran down the steps, and the door began to close behind us. The engine hum grew louder, and the spacecraft suddenly shot high into the air. The spacecraft's shiny metal surface gleamed brilliantly in the sun. It lurched forward and sped away.

Meghan and I were alone in the field.

If Alpena was going to be saved from the Globblings, it was going to be up to us.

15

We had no idea where to start . . . but we knew we'd better start fast! I mean . . . how does somebody go about finding a big red blob in Alpena? We sure weren't going to be able to ask anyone!

"Let's start down by the water," Meghan said. "That's where the Globblings are coming from. Maybe we can catch them as they leave the lake."

"Good idea," I said. "That way, we might be able to stop them before they get into the city."

I started to walk.

"Wait," Meghan said. "We need to know how to use these things." She waved the photron laser pistol.

"Another good idea," I said. "Let's try—" I paused, looking around the empty field. "Let's try a tree." I aimed the photron laser at a tree, held my arm steady a moment, and fired.

The whole tree blew up! Bark and branches and leaves and pieces of the tree were everywhere!

"Wow!" Meghan said. "My turn!"

Meghan held out her photron laser gun, aimed at a tree, and fired.

Boom!

"Hey, that's cool!" she cried.

"I just hope our aim is that good with the Globblings," I said.

I stuffed my photron laser in my pocket. The handle stuck out a bit, but it wasn't really noticeable. Meghan put hers in her pocket, too.

We walked out of the woods and came to a road. It was US-23, and I knew right where we were. It didn't take us long to walk downtown and to the lake.

The day was sunny. It was late afternoon, and there were a lot of kids playing down by the water. Not too many were swimming, though. Being that it was early summer, the water was still a little cold. But there were a couple of real little kids splashing about in the shallows. Little kids don't seem to be bothered by the cold water.

We walked along the water's edge, our eyes scanning the surface of the big lake. Lake Huron is huge. It's so big that you can't see land on the other side. It's more like an ocean than it is a lake!

"See anything?" Meghan whispered.

"Not yet," I said.

We kept looking.

"What if they're already in the city?" Meghan asked.

"Well, they might be. We just have to be on the lookout."

We walked farther. Suddenly Meghan's hand shot up, pointing to the sky.

"Mark! There's one! Right there!"

She was right! Far out over the lake, I could

barely make out a flying red blob in the sky.

But as we watched, we could tell that it was coming.

It was headed for Alpena.

I pulled out my photron laser.

"Not here!" Meghan said. "Someone will see us and think we've gone crazy!"

Meghan was right. We would have to duck off into the bushes or hide somewhere.

"Over there," I said, pointing to a small boathouse near the water. "We can go behind that building."

We ran to the boathouse and ducked behind it. From behind the structure, no one could see us. We were out of sight.

Out over the water, the Globbling was approaching quickly. I drew my photron laser and aimed. Meghan pulled hers out and aimed it, too.

"Just in case you miss," she said.

"I'm not going to miss," I answered. I took one more second to aim . . . then pulled the trigger.

The beam of light tore through the sky — and

went right past the Globbling.

I missed!

But the Globbling saw the laser go by. It saw where the laser had come from.

The Globbling saw us, and with lightning speed, he attacked!

He was coming for us!

16

I had no idea those things could move that fast! The Globbling came at us like a rocket.

Meghan was still clutching her photron laser, and she held her aim . . . and fired. The thin beam of light shot through the blue sky.

It was a direct hit!

The creature exploded in mid-air. Red blobs rain down upon the water.

"Nice going, Meg!" I shouted. "That was a great shot!"

Meghan smiled, but it was a worried smile.

"It scares me that they can move so fast like that," she said.

It scared me, too, but I didn't say so.

"Come on," Meghan said. "Let's keep looking."

We emerged from behind the boathouse and walked along the shore. I couldn't take my eyes off the sky. If those Globblings could move that fast, we'd really have to be on our guards. I sure didn't want to be eaten by a Globbling!

We didn't have to walk far. Coming out of the water, not far from us, was another one. This one wasn't flying, but it wasn't really walking, either. It was just kind of trudging through the water toward the shore.

It was hideous looking. It was just this big red blob that was shaped like a monster. It looked just like the one we had seen under water.

This time, we didn't have a chance to run anywhere. We were already too close to the alien, and if we didn't shoot now, he might get away.

Or worse—he might get *us!*

There was no time to spare. I drew my photron laser and fired.

The Globbling exploded!

"Hey, I think you're catching on with that thing," Meghan smirked. I just shook my head. Meghan's playful ribbing was something I was used to.

"Come on," I said. "Let's keep looking."

We were walking along the shore when suddenly, I felt a tug at my waist.

"Got it!" I heard someone yell. I spun, fearing the worst. I already knew what had happened.

A small boy, about five years old, had snatched my photron laser!

17

"I got your squirt-gun, I got your squirt-gun," he sang, waving the weapon about.

This was dangerous! The kid thought that he was playing with a squirt-gun . . . when it was actually a very dangerous weapon!

"Give me that back, you little brat!" I said.

He took off running! Oh no!

Meghan and I chased him through the sand.

"I got your squirt-gun, I got your squirt-gun," the boy continued singing. He couldn't run very fast and it was pretty easy to catch up with him.

But as we did, the kid spun around and pointed the gun at me!

"I'm going to get you all wet!" he giggled.

"No!" Meghan shouted in horror. "You don't understand! That's *not* a squirt-gun!"

The boy just stood there, aiming the gun at us.

"*I got your squirt-gun, I got your squirt-gun,*" he repeated.

This was a recipe for disaster!

"Please," I pleaded, extending my hand. "Please give it back. It doesn't belong to you. And it's very dangerous."

The boy continued to wave the gun back and forth. I didn't dare risk trying to grab it from him. It might go off, and someone might get hurt.

Or *worse!*

"I got your squirt-gun, I got your—"

"Jimmy! Jimmy, you give that back this instant!" It was the little brat's Mom!

The little boy turned his head, and it was the break I needed. I lunged forward and snapped the gun out of his hand.

Meanwhile, the kid's mother was walking toward us, scolding her son.

"That was a very, very, naughty thing to do!" she said. She looked at Meghan and I. "I'm very sorry that he took your squirt gun," she said, taking her son by the hand.

"No problem," I answered.

The woman led the boy away.

"Whew," Meghan said. "That was close."

"I think we'd better be careful with these things," I said. "If they fall into the wrong hands, anything could happen."

"Mark, look!" Meghan suddenly shouted, pointing toward the band shell in Bay View park. What I saw made me cringe.

They were big.

They were red.

They were Globblings.

They had reached the city!

18

The Globblings were standing on the other side of the band shell.

Had anyone seen them yet? Or worse—had *they* seen anyone, yet?

Brothron said that Globblings will eat just about anything.

Including people!

"We have to stop them," Meghan said.

We ran from the shore, ducking behind trees, hoping that we weren't spotted by the aliens. We would have to be careful.

"Oh my gosh!" Meghan whispered. *"One of them is eating something!"*

Oh no! Were we too late?

There was only one way to find out. I drew my photron laser.

"Come on!" I said. "We've got to stop them!"

We sprang through the grass in a full run toward the Globblings. As soon as we were close enough, I began firing.

A hit! My first shot destroyed the Globbling, and a cloud of red, mushy debris splattered all over the place.

The other Globbling turned. He was eating—

A bicycle! The Globbling held the bike in his hands, chomping on the handlebars!

Brothron was right . . . Globblings *would* eat just about anything!

"I'll get him!" Meghan cried. She drew her photron laser just as the Globbling began to charge us. The beam of light struck the Globbling, and it exploded.

"What a team!" I said, slapping Meghan's hand in a high-five.

But we knew it wasn't over. Brothron himself didn't know how many Globblings had invaded earth. There might be many, many more.

I stuffed the photron laser back into my pocket.

"Let's have a look downtown," I said. Meghan put her laser gun in her pocket and we walked up to Chisolm Street.

Alpena isn't a real big city, and I figured if the Globblings had started to invade, word would get out pretty fast. People would panic, and there would be a lot of confusion. Everyone would be a lot better off if we could fend off the Globblings without anyone in Alpena knowing about them.

We walked around downtown for a while, peeking behind buildings and houses, but we didn't see any signs of the space aliens. We even walked back through Bay View park and down by Thunder Bay Shores marina.

"I think our chances are better down by the water on the other side of the park," Meghan said.

I agreed. "Let's head back there," I said.

Suddenly a hand grabbed my shoulder and

spun me around!

I was face to face . . . not with a space alien . . . *but with Greg Daniels!*

19

"Hey, chicken . . . I've been looking for you."

A lump formed in my throat. I took a step back, and so did Meghan.

Greg took a step forward.

"Thought you could get away from me, huh?" he sneered, pounding his fist into the palm of his other hand.

"Leave us alone!" Meghan demanded.

"And just what are *you* going to do about it, little girl?"

"Who are you calling 'little'?" Meghan demanded. She was mad!

"Buzz off you geeky little twerp," Greg said

to her. "I'm busy with the chicken."

That was the last straw for Meghan. She was mad enough that Greg had called her 'little', but when he called her a 'geeky twerp'—well, that was just too much. She hauled off and kicked Greg right in the shin!

"Oooowwww!!" Greg howled, doubling over and grabbing his leg.

"Run!" Meghan shouted.

She didn't have to tell me twice!

We darted around Greg, leaving him hopping on one leg, holding his other leg with both hands.

"Ooooowwww!!" Greg howled. "Now you've done it! Just wait 'till I find you! Now you're *both* going to get it!"

Our feet pounded the pavement as we put more and more distance between ourselves and Greg Daniels.

"Remind . . . me," I said between breaths as we ran, "never . . . to . . . pick . . . a . . . fight . . . with . . . you!"

We ran as fast as we could, through downtown and behind a grocery store. When I was sure that Greg hadn't followed us, we stopped.

"Good going!" I said, my lungs heaving. "Now Greg is going to kill me *and* you!"

"Well, he deserved it," Meghan said sharply. "He's the one who . . . oh gosh! *LOOK!*"

I turned and followed her gaze.

The little boy that had swiped my photron laser gun was playing in a sand box.

And creeping up right behind him was a Globbling!

20

The little boy wouldn't stand a chance. He was playing in the sand, completely lost in his own world. Meanwhile, the creature was getting closer and closer, its arms spread wide, ready to lunge at the boy.

Suddenly the brat turned and saw the alien! He dropped the pail he was playing with, but he was too afraid to move! He just stood there as the awful alien lurched closer and closer. I saw the brat's mouth open as if he were about to let out a scream, but no sound came out.

There was only one thing I could do . . . and I didn't hesitate.

In one swift motion I drew the photron laser, dropped to my knees, and fired. Meghan did the same, only she held her fire in case I missed. Then she would shoot.

But she didn't have to.

The laser struck the space alien, and he exploded in a cloud of gooey jelly. Blobs of red splattered all over the sand and the grass. It looked like someone had broken a giant jar of strawberry jam.

The boy turned and looked at us. His eyes were as big as golf balls, and his mouth still hung open. Meghan and I stood up, quickly putting the photron lasers back into our pockets. That had been a close one. I mean . . . the kid *was* a brat, but that didn't mean I wanted him to be eaten by a Globbling!

The little boy took off running. He ran up the beach and through the grass to his mother, who was sitting at a picnic table in the shade. She was reading a book, and she put it down as the boy approached. She was completely unaware of any danger.

"Mommy! Mommy!" the little boy cried, his

arms outstretched. "Monster! Monster!"

"Oh, for heaven's sake," his mother replied, taking him into her arms. "There's no such thing as monsters."

"Mommy! It was a monster!" The boy pointed toward Meghan and I. "They killed it with their guns!"

His mother looked up at us. We were still a ways away from her, but we could see her face. I decided to play along.

I pulled the gun out of my pocket and waved it in the air.

"Yeah, it was a monster, all right," I yelled. "But we took care of it with our squirt guns. You're safe. No more monsters around here!" I gave her my best Boy Scout salute, and returned the gun to my pocket.

The boy's mother smiled. "See?" she said to her son. "Those nice people got rid of the monster. You can go and play now."

But the kid refused to go anywhere, and instead snuggled closer to his mother. I think the sight of the Globbling scared him so much that he didn't even want to play anymore.

I guess I couldn't blame him!

Meghan and I continued walking along the sandy shore of Lake Huron.

Looking for space aliens.

We didn't have to look very far.

21

It was in the sky. Meghan saw it first.

"Look!" she cried, pointing up and squinting in the afternoon sun.

The Globbling was very high in the sky. It was so high that it was just a red dot beneath a canopy of blue.

And it was huge!

"There's no way we can hit that thing," I said. "He's too far away."

"But we've got to try!" Meghan pleaded.

She was right.

We both pulled out our photron lasers and fired.

We missed by a mile. He was just too far away.

"We've got to follow him!" I said, breaking into a run. Meghan started running, and we bounded through the sand, across thick grass, and onto hard pavement. It was tough going, because we had to watch where we were running and, at the same time, we had to watch the Globbling high in the sky. Once I almost tripped and fell.

"He's coming down!" Meghan shouted from behind me. I looked up.

Sure enough, the Globbling was lower in the sky.

"As soon as he gets low enough, one of us will have to shoot him with the laser gun!" I shouted back. "Don't let him get away!

We ran faster, snapping our heads upward to follow the Globbling, then quickly glancing down at the pavement beneath our feet.

The Globbling looked like it was headed for the forest . . . the same forest, in fact, where we had found the spacecraft earlier in the day. Soon, we were running through the woods.

"Don't lose him!" Meghan shouted from behind me.

"I won't!" I shouted back.

I had a difficult time running. Branches kept smacking me in the face. I had to duck and swerve a lot to keep from getting scratched up.

I could still make out the Globbling in the sky. He was much closer to the ground now, but it would have been impossible to shoot the space creature through the thick tree branches.

"STOP!!!" Meghan suddenly screamed.

I came to a halt, and turned around, facing her.

"What's wrong?" I panted. Sweat had formed on my forehead, and I wiped it away with the back of my hand.

Meghan pointed, and I looked in the direction of her outstretched arm.

I froze.

A chill shot down my spine like a rocket.

It was the spaceship. Brothron's spaceship.

It was in a small field—

Surrounded by Globblings!

It was awful.

Worse.

It was a *disaster!*

The spaceship was surrounded by ten Globblings . . . ten *huge* Globblings . . . *and they were trying to eat the spaceship!*

We had to act fast. If we didn't do something right now, this very second, well . . . there was no telling what might happen!

"*OPEN FIRE!*" I shouted to Meghan. We both drew our photron lasers and dropped to our knees.

Laser blasts flew through the air! Globblings began to explode, and red goo began to splatter all over the place!

"Be careful not to hit the ship!" Meghan shouted above the roaring lasers.

A couple Globblings saw where we were and charged. Meghan shot two of them, and I got one just as it had taken flight. The Globbling that we had spotted in the air had landed, but a quick laser blast from my gun took care of him.

There was only one left. He was on the other side of the spaceship, so we didn't have a clear shot at him.

Suddenly, the creature took off into the air! Its huge wings began beating rapidly as it swooped up over the craft.

"Get him!" I shouted. "Get him before he gets away!"

Meghan and I fired wildly, but the creature was too fast. He darted through branches and disappeared over the treetops.

We had lost him!

"Come on," I said to Meghan. "We'll have to find him later. Let's make sure Brothron is okay." Meghan jumped up and followed me.

We sprinted across the field toward the

spaceship. The whole battle had taken less than a minute. There was sticky red goo on the ground, on the trees, on the spaceship . . . everywhere. It was really gross.

"Brothron!" I shouted. "Brothron! Are you all right?!?!?"

The door of the spaceship wasn't open, and there was no noise from inside. I pounded on the side of the craft.

"Brothron!" I cried again. "Brothron . . . are you okay?!?!?"

Suddenly, we heard a shuffling sound from inside the craft! The door began to open.

Brothron!

He still had his silver space suit on, but his helmet was now completely off. He looked . . . well . . . *strange*. Like you'd expect a space alien to look. His head was really wide and he didn't have any ears. Just small holes where each ear should be.

But he looked happy to see us!

"Excellent job!" he exclaimed. "They overtook me in the air. There were so many, I couldn't shoot them all. I had to make an emergency landing. If you hadn't come along when you did, I would've been in *real* trouble."

"What happened?" Meghan asked. "Did you find their spaceship?"

"Well, sort of," Brothron said, taking a step down the stairs.

Suddenly, he stumbled! I had to reach out and catch him before he fell!

"What's wrong?!?!" I asked, steadying him on the stairs. "Are you all right?"

"Oh, dear. I thought I was. I got bumped around in the spaceship while I was trying to get away from the Globblings. I think I hurt my leg and my arm."

"Well, come and sit down for a minute," Meghan said, and we helped Brothron down the stairs and to the grass. I don't think he could have walked very far without our help.

"Tell us what happened," I said.

"I was in Lake Huron," he began. "I was getting close to their ship. I knew I was. All of a sudden, there they were! A whole swarm of them! They attacked my craft before I had a chance to do anything. The jolt was so sudden and so strong that it broke my seat belt! I fell right out of my chair and the force threw me across the cockpit. That's how I got hurt. I barely made it back here to the field without crashing."

"You were lucky you were able to get away," Meghan said.

"Yes, I was," Brothron agreed, nodding. "And thanks to you, the Globblings on land are gone."

"Not quite," Meghan answered. "One got away. We have to go get him."

"Well, at the moment," Brothron said, "we have a bigger problem. There are still Globblings in their spaceship, and maybe some in Lake Huron. They've turned on a homing device in their spacecraft. It's a strong radio frequency that goes far out into space. Right now, their ship is transmitting a radio signal back to Globbla."

"So?" I asked.

"So, it's letting all of the other Globblings know that there is food here. By this time tomorrow, there might be a thousand Globbling spaceships invading your planet."

A thousand Globbling spaceships!

Oh no!!

23

My mind was racing.

A thousand Globbling spaceships?!?!? That might mean hundreds of thousands of Globblings! Alpena would be destroyed! The whole *planet* would be wiped out!

"We've got to stop them!" I cried. "We can't let them attack! We just can't!"

"The only thing we can do is destroy their ship," Brothron said. "But I'm afraid, in my condition, I just can't fly."

I didn't hesitate to volunteer.

"I'll fly your spaceship," I said, leaping to my feet. "You can show me. I'll fly it."

Meghan looked at me like I was out of my mind. Even Brothron looked at me like I was absolutely crazy!

"You've got to be kidding," he said. "It takes years of training to learn to fly a spacecraft. Especially this one."

"Well, we don't have years," I pleaded. "In fact, we might not have until tomorrow."

"No," Brothron said, shaking his head. "I cannot let you fly it. It would be too dangerous. You have no idea what you're doing."

"You can show me," I persisted. "You can tell me exactly what to do, and I'll do it. I promise."

"Mark's right," Meghan agreed quietly. "If we don't find the Globbling spacecraft and stop that radio signal, it will be too late. Mark *has* to fly your spaceship, if you can't. It's our last . . . and *only* . . . chance."

Brothron thought about it for a moment.

"I suppose," he began, "if you do *exactly* what I tell you to do. Nothing else."

"Let's go," I said. "We don't have a second to spare."

Meghan and I helped Brothron up. He was quite heavy, and he had a difficult time standing. I think he was hurt even more than he said he was.

After some struggling, we were able to get Brothron back on the ship. He sat in the co-pilot's seat. I took my position in the pilot's seat, and Meghan sat behind me. She buckled herself in. I tried to buckle myself in but—

The belt was broken! I forgot! Brothron said that the seat belt had snapped when the Globblings attacked his ship. That was how he got hurt. The torn ends lay limp, dangling from the seat. I was really going to have to be careful.

Brothron looked at the broken belt and shook his head.

"That's my fault," he said. "I was supposed to have this thing in for its six billion mile check-up last week."

Six billion miles?!?! Man . . . this is one alien that really gets around!

Brothron walked me through the steps to get the spacecraft started. It was really complicated, and I had a hard time remembering everything.

There were hundreds of buttons and levers and blinking lights and gauges and dials and switches. I began to think that there was no way I could fly this thing.

But I had to. I had to — or *else!*

"Okay," Brothron said. "Push that green button and flick the red switch at the same time."

Click. Click-click.

A quiet hum arose through the spacecraft.

"Now," Brothron continued, "press that red button above you."

I reached up and pressed the button.

Click.

The hyper engines roared to life.

"Put your hands on the throttle and ease the lever back," Brothron instructed.

When I did, I felt the whole spaceship shudder.

Then it lifted off the ground!

I was doing it! I was flying a spaceship!

24

This was too cool!

The spaceship went straight up in the air. Within a few seconds, we were over the treetops!

"You're doing it, Mark!" Meghan cheered. "You're really doing it! You're flying the spaceship!"

I have to admit, even though the whole world was in danger, I really *did* enjoy flying the spaceship. I couldn't wait to tell my friends!

But, then again, who would believe me? Who would believe that Mark Blackburn, an average kid from Alpena, Michigan, actually had a chance to fly an alien spaceship?

Well, at least Meghan would believe me. She had to—she was here!

"Now," Brothron said, after we had risen above the trees, "gently shift the lever to the left."

As I did, I felt the craft begin to turn.

"And now," Brothron said, "press the red button on the lever, and slowly push the lever forward."

The spacecraft began to move forward! I was doing it! I was really flying an alien spaceship! The ground was far below me, and I could see streets and trees and houses whooshing by faster and faster.

"That's it," Brothron encouraged. "You're doing fine."

I pushed the lever forward a bit more and the spacecraft began to go even faster. Man, I wished I had one of these of my own! It was a lot more fun than my bicycle!

"All right, Mark!" Meghan cheered from the seat behind me.

I have to admit, it felt pretty good. When I

looked down, I could see all of Alpena! I could see the city and all the streets, and even cars and trucks.

And Lake Huron . . . which was where we were headed.

"Are we going to go into the lake?" Meghan asked.

"Yes," Brothron answered. "We have to find the Globbling spaceship. I think I have an idea where it might be. And we can always use the radio locator to help us find it."

"The radio locator?" I asked. "What's that?"

"It's a device that listens for radio waves," Brothron explained. "It can tell us which direction they're coming from. So if the Globblings are transmitting a radio signal, and I'm sure they are, we'll be able to find their ship."

The ground below us fell away, and now all we could see was water. It was beautiful and crystal blue. Far away, I could see puffy white clouds on the horizon. I could even see a big ship in the water! It looked like it was a freighter. We see them a lot.

"Now, press the yellow button on the lever, and pull back very gently," Brothron instructed.

When I did, the ship began to dive. Not very much at first, but the more I pulled the lever back, the steeper we dived.

"Ease up just a little bit," Brothron said. "Since you don't have a seat belt, we'll have to enter the water slowly. Try pushing the pedal on the floor with your foot."

As I did, I could feel the spaceship begin to slow very quickly. The pedal must have been a brake of some sort.

As we began to sink closer and closer to the surface of Lake Huron, I pressed the pedal a bit harder. We were now moving very slowly.

"What's that?!?" Meghan suddenly shouted, pointing to something in the water. I looked, but I didn't see anything.

"Where?" I asked.

But she didn't have to tell me.

I gasped.

Meghan gasped.

Even Brothron gasped.

It was a Globbling. Not just any

Globbling—but a *giant* Globbling—the size of a house!

He was coming out of the water—and he was headed straight for us!

25

I don't think I've ever seen such an awful looking creature in my life! The Globbling was red and fat and had arms and legs and wings. It looked like it was made out of jelly!

But I wasn't fooled. Even though it *looked* like it was made out of jelly, I knew that the space alien was dangerous.

Very dangerous.

"Quick!" Brothron ordered. "Fire a photron laser rocket!"

Huh? I didn't know how to do that!

"On your far right!" Brothron shouted. *"Press the red switch down!"*

I followed Brothron's orders and reached for

the switch. A loud *beep-beep-beep-beep* came from somewhere inside the cabin. I looked out the windshield to see the Globbling quickly approaching.

"Now, press the blue button on the throttle!" Brothron instructed. *"Hurry!"*

As I did, the whole ship shuddered, and a brilliant blast of light engulfed everything in front of the windshield! I could see the strong beam of light heading for the Globbling.

Closer . . . almost there —

Bingo!

The Globbling exploded into billions of red blobs, scattering all over the water. It was incredible!

"That was close," I whispered.

"Too close," Meghan said, breathing a sigh of relief from behind me.

Below us, we were approaching the surface of Lake Huron.

"Okay," Brothron said. "Listen carefully. Do you see the row of switches on the panel above you?"

I glanced up. "Yes," I said.

"Flip all of them to the 'on' position," Brothron instructed.

I flipped the switches.

"Now," Brothron continued, "gently ease the spaceship down to the surface."

I pulled back on the throttle lever, and the spacecraft came to rest on the surface. We were floating! Or, at least, it seemed like we were floating.

"There's a yellow dial on the right side of the panel," Brothron said. "That's the automatic pressure adjustment. Turn it all the way to the right."

Once again, I followed Brothron's orders.

"Now," Brothron said confidently, "let's go destroy the Globbling spaceship."

I gently guided the throttle lever forward, and the spacecraft began to sink. It was a weird feeling! The water kept rising as the spacecraft sank lower and lower. In a few seconds, the water was up to the windshield. Soon, the craft was completely under water!

Everything was a misty blue. As the spacecraft dove deeper and deeper, the water became darker.

"There's a white switch above you that will turn on the spiral energy lights," Brothron said. "Do you see it?"

I looked up and saw the switch, answering Brothron by reaching up and clicking the switch. Suddenly, the waters in front of us were lit up brightly.

"But," Meghan wondered aloud, "if we have our lights on, won't the Globblings see us?" she asked.

"That's a chance we have to take," Brothron said. "Mark . . . turn on the radio transmission censor. It's a black button right in front of you, just below the windshield."

When I flipped the lever, I heard a strange pinging sound.

"That's from the Globbling's ship, all right. They're sending out a radio signal. We don't have a lot of time. Let's see if we can pick up their ship on the grid."

From where he was, Brothron could reach a small button that lit up a green-colored screen. I could still hear the strange pinging sound, but now a white dot appeared on the green screen. Every time I heard a ping, the dot blinked.

"There she is," Brothron said, pointing to the blinking white dot. "That's the Globbling spaceship. Set a course straight for that dot."

This all seemed so very easy. Fly the spaceship, destroy a Globbling, and go into Lake Huron. Now all we needed to do was find the Globbling's spaceship, blast it with a super-charged photron laser, and we'd be done. Alpena . . . and the whole world . . . would be saved.

Man, was I wrong . . . and I was about to find out just how wrong I was!

#

We were about to crash.

Oh, I didn't know it at that moment, but I sure found out quickly!

The spaceship had been cruising along fine. We saw a few fish, but so far, no Globblings.

The rock formation came out of nowhere. One moment we were moving along, watching the dark sea in front of us . . . and the next moment, a huge boulder was in our path!

"Turn! Turn! Turn!" Brothron's robot-like voice shouted.

I grabbed the lever and pulled it all the way over to the left. The spacecraft responded quickly, snapping sideways—

—but it was too late!

"Hold on!" Brothron shouted. *"Hold on tight! We're going to hit!"*

I let go of the lever and grabbed the seat, holding on for life. Boy . . . I sure didn't make a very good spaceship pilot! I raised my hands to cover my face. We were goners!

BAM!

We hit!

The force of the impact knocked me to the floor, and sent me sprawling to the back of the craft. I steadied myself against a wall, then I climbed to my knees.

Lights began to flash and warning sirens began to sound. I could feel the ship tumbling, sliding sideways, out of control.

Suddenly, there was another crash as the spaceship hit the bottom. The jolt once again knocked me down, and I tumbled to the floor, tossed about in the spacecraft. I hit my head on the bottom of one of the chairs, but luckily, not very hard.

The spacecraft stopped moving.

The lights went out.

The engines hummed for a few more seconds, then stopped. Everything was black, and I couldn't see an inch in front of my face.

We were alive. We were alive, but we were stranded. The spacecraft had crashed . . . four hundred feet below the surface of Lake Huron.

27

We were in total darkness. Total darkness, at the bottom of Lake Huron. I have never before felt so helpless in my entire life. Not even when Greg Daniels had been chasing me!

"Meghan?" I said. "Are you okay?"

"I . . . I think so," she answered from behind me.

"Brothron?" I asked. "How about you?"

"Oh, I'm fine, I'm fine," he replied. "The problem isn't with us . . . it's with the spaceship."

Everything was really quiet for a moment. Then I heard Brothron shuffling in his seat.

Suddenly a light turned on! There was a dim light coming from above us. It wasn't very bright, but I could see well enough to make out the shadows of Brothron and Meghan.

"Thank goodness," Brothron said. "The emergency power still works."

"Man, I'm really sorry about this," I said. And I was. Once I broke our neighbor's window with a baseball, and I was really sorry for that, too.

But this was a lot different!

Brothron unbuckled his seat belt, and I helped him up. He was still hurting, but he seemed to be able to move around better. He was checking gauges and dials and switches.

"Uh-huh," he said to himself. "Okay . . . all right . . . ." He flipped a couple switches, but nothing happened. "No, that's not good," he said.

My heart sank.

"Oh, but *that's* good," he said, looking at a small glowing screen before him.

My heart leapt.

"Oh, but then again, that's not good there,"

he muttered, staring at a panel of switches on the wall.

My heart sank again. Up, down, up, down. It felt like my heart was playing leapfrog.

Brothron inspected the instrument panel, saying nothing. I was certain that we were goners.

"Ah-hah!" he exclaimed suddenly. "I think we can get out of here!"

My heart leapt again.

"Do you think so?" Meghan asked, her voice full of hope. "Do you really think so?"

"Yes, I do," Brothron answered. And with that, he flipped a switch.

I crossed my fingers.

Suddenly—a noise! The engines! I heard the engines roar to life!

"Well, the ship has suffered some damage, but I think it will survive. And so will we."

I don't think I have ever been happier in my entire life.

"Let's get going again," Brothron said. He sat back down in his chair and buckled himself in.

"Don't . . . don't *you* want to pilot this thing?" I asked. "I mean . . . I've already crashed it once. I don't want to do it again."

"You'll do fine," Brothron said. "Besides, I don't think I can fly it. You'll do just fine. We'll just have to go slow."

I took my place once again in the pilot's seat.

"You'll be great," Meghan said urging me on. It was nice of her to say that, but I wasn't so sure of myself.

Regardless, we were off again, with Brothron giving me instructions of what to do.

But this time, we went a lot slower.

"Okay, slow down even more," Brothron ordered. "We're getting close." We had only been searching for a few minutes.

I glanced at the green screen in front of Brothron. The dot was almost in the center of the grid. Brothron said that when the dot was in the center of the screen, we would find the alien spacecraft.

And we did.

In the murky depths, a large, silvery ball seemed to come from out of nowhere, looming above us like the rock formation that we had crashed into. Only this time, we were going real slow, and we weren't in danger of hitting it.

It was huge. It was ten times bigger than Brothron's spacecraft. But there weren't any blinking lights or anything. It looked just like a giant steel ball.

"Okay," Brothron said quietly. "Let's take care of that Globbling spacecraft."

I slowed the spaceship to a stop. Once again, I prepared to fire the super photron laser.

"Steady," Brothron said. "Be steady . . . that's it . . . okay — *fire!*"

28

I pressed the button.

Click.

Nothing.

I pressed the button again.

Click.

The photron lasers! They didn't work! They must've been damaged in the crash!

This was just not my day.

"Brothron!" I shouted. "The lasers! They're not working!"

Brothron leaned over, inspecting the control panel. He flicked a couple of switches, but nothing worked. The photron lasers would not respond.

Then Brothron asked me something that made my jaw drop.

"Can you swim?" His big, black eyes stared at me.

"Say *what?!?!?!*" I replied.

"Can you *swim?*"

"Well . . . yeah," I stammered. But what was he thinking? We were four hundred feet below the surface!

"You'll have to do this from outside the ship," Brothron said.

"But . . . I can't go outside the spacecraft!" I protested. "We're too deep! I'd be crushed by the water pressure!"

"Not true," Brothron said, shaking his big, round head.

Somehow, I just knew he was going to say that.

"The ship is pressurized, and the suits are made to withstand pressures far greater than this. It will be just like wearing a heavy set of clothing. You can probably fit into my spare."

"Into one of *your* spacesuits?" I asked.

"Yes," Brothron said. "Help me up."

Meghan unbuckled herself and stood up to help Brothron, and I leaned over to steady him. We helped him walk to the other side of the craft. He pressed a couple buttons on the wall and a panel slid open. There were a half-dozen shelves in the wall. One of them had a shiny, silver suit neatly folded. There was also a helmet on another shelf, the same kind of helmet that Brothron had been wearing.

"Hurry," Brothron said. "We have no time to waste." He pulled out the suit and handed it to me.

It was at this time that I pinched my arm to wake myself up. There was no way this could be happening! I knew I had to be dreaming.

But I wasn't. I pinched myself, but I didn't wake up. I was already awake.

I knew it would be useless to protest any more, and besides . . . Brothron knew what he was doing. If he said that I'd be okay underwater in the suit, then I'm sure I would be fine.

At least, that's what I *told* myself.

"The suit is designed for protection in any

kind of element," Brothron said. "You could even walk through fire with one of these suits, and not even feel the heat."

Somehow, that didn't make me feel any better.

I pulled out the photron laser gun and handed it to Meghan while I climbed into the suit. The suit wasn't as thick as I thought it would be. It felt like I was putting on a heavy denim jumpsuit.

Meghan laughed. "It looks like a Halloween costume," she giggled.

I placed the helmet over my head while Brothron helped to fasten up the suit, all the while explaining what I was to do.

"In the back of this craft, there is a small door that opens from the floor. The ship is pressurized so that when the door slides open, no water will come in. You'll be able to use the photron laser pistol to destroy the alien spacecraft."

"These things work underwater?" I asked, nodding toward the photron laser gun in Meghan's hand.

Brothron nodded to me without speaking, and Meghan handed me back the laser gun. "Good luck," she said.

"Thanks," I replied.

Out of the corner of my eye, I caught a movement from beyond the windshield.

"Brothron! Look!" I shouted.

A door was opening on the alien spaceship!

29

"Hurry!" Brothron ordered. "You must go now!"

He pressed a button on a panel of blinking lights and suddenly a door on the floor slid back, exposing a dark, watery hole. Water sloshed and splashed, but it didn't come into the ship.

"All you'll need to do is aim at the ship and fire the photron laser pistol," Brothron said. "Even that small laser gun is capable of destroying the entire Globbling spacecraft. *Hurry!*"

It was now or never.

I nodded to Meghan, and she nodded back,

but I could see the fear in her eyes. She was afraid for me.

Matter of fact . . . *I* was afraid for me! But I couldn't let that stop me. Regardless of whether I was scared or not, there was something far more important that I had to think about.

Destroying the Globbling spacecraft.

I walked over to the open door on the floor, took a step forward, and dropped into the water feet-first.

It was an eerie feeling, being in water so deep. Everything around me was pitch black, except where the lights of the spacecraft were. I could see the alien spacecraft, and I could see the door opening more and more.

Were more Globblings coming out?

I decided not to wait to find out. I swam away from Brothron's spaceship so I could get a better shot at the alien craft.

Swimming in the suit was very clumsy, and holding onto the photron laser gun made moving about even *more* difficult.

The door on the Globbling's ship kept opening farther and farther. I didn't want to be around to see what was coming out!

Steadying myself on the silty bottom of Lake Huron, I leveled the photron laser gun at the ship and aimed for the open door.

I pulled the trigger.

The beam of light shot through the water with lightning speed. It was a direct hit!

But—

Nothing happened! I waited, my mind frantic. Had I done something wrong?

Suddenly, the Globbling spacecraft began to shudder and shake. I could feel the rumble and hear the thundering sound through the water.

The alien craft *imploded!* It didn't explode outward . . . it exploded *inward!*

Suddenly, it all made sense to me. Of course the craft wouldn't explode! We were too deep and the water pressure was too great! By shooting the photron laser through the door of the craft, it destroyed the Globbling ship . . . *from the inside out!* The blast from the photron laser weakened the craft, and it was crushed under the enormous water pressure!

There was debris everywhere. The

Globbling spacecraft had been completely demolished! A large cloud of debris slowly floated through the water. Alpena—and the whole world—had been saved!

Or so I had thought.

I forgot that there was still a Globbling running around the city.

I was about to find out that our work wasn't over, after all.

30

I swam back to the spacecraft and slipped beneath it. When I popped my head up into the craft, Brothron and Meghan were all smiles.

"You did it!" Meghan exclaimed. "You really did it!"

I climbed back into the craft. Water splashed on the floor and dripped from my suit as I stood up. I unfastened the helmet and lifted it off my head. I looked at Brothron.

He was smiling, but there was something behind that smile that told me we weren't quite finished yet.

Meghan helped me out of the suit and

Brothron sat back down. When I glanced over at him, he looked very tired, like he was about to go to sleep.

"Brothron?" I said. "What's wrong?" I folded up the dripping spacesuit and set it on the floor next to my seat. I sat down, and so did Meghan.

"I am afraid I am not feeling at all well," Brothron said. "I must return back to Vargondan immediately. Otherwise . . . ."

He didn't have to finish. Meghan and I both knew what he meant. Brothron was dying, and unless he returned to his planet now, it would be too late.

"But what about the Globbling?" I asked. "One is still somewhere in Alpena."

"Yes," Brothron agreed, "but you must take care of it on your own." His voice sounded raspy and weak.

"But . . . but how can you pilot your spacecraft?" Meghan asked.

Good question.

"I can program the ship to fly back to Vargondan," Brothron answered. "I won't need to steer the ship. I can just put the coordinates into the craft's computer, and it will take me home." He closed his eyes.

Brothron was fading, and fast.

"Let's go," I said to Meghan. I tried to remember everything I needed to do to pilot the spacecraft. Meghan helped buckle Brothron into his seat, then she sat down and buckled herself in.

"Hang on," I said, and the craft slowly began to lurch forward. I pulled the throttle back and the ship began to climb, slowly at first, and then faster as I turned the throttle. The dark waters around us lightened as we drew near the surface.

Suddenly, the craft exploded out of the water and into the sunshine. The brilliant blue sky filled the windshield. Thin rivers of water streamed down the glass.

Boy, was I glad to be out of the water!

I turned the craft, and we headed toward land. I must say, Alpena sure is beautiful from the air. I had never seen the city from this high in the sky before.

We were silent as the spacecraft sped toward land. A few boats dotted the water below, and the sun shined brightly on the glistening water.

"I'm going to find that field where we were before," I said.

The ship sailed over Alpena. I could see cars, trucks, even a few people. But we were so high in the air that the people looked like tiny ants.

"Over there," Meghan suddenly said, pointing. She had spotted the field.

I steered the craft in the direction of the large meadow, and slowly began to descend to the ground.

Brothron remained silent, saving his strength. He looked like he was really hurting. I really hoped that he would be able to make it back to Vargondan in time.

The landing was a little bumpy, I must admit. Being new to this spaceship thing, I hadn't had too much time to practice my landings. The craft jolted about, rocking and shaking as I clumsily landed the spaceship in the tall, thick grass. We hit the ground with a heavy thud, jarring all of us in our seats.

"Sorry about that," I said.

Brothron flicked a couple of switches, and the whirring engines died off.

Meghan quickly unfastened her safety belt and stood up. We both helped Brothron to the control seat.

"Are you sure you're going to be okay?" I asked. Brothron looked like he was half asleep.

He managed a smile. "I'll be fine," he said quietly.

Slowly, he began setting switches and dials. He typed something into what looked like a computer keyboard, then flicked on a couple more switches.

"Go," he said. "You have work to do. But you must promise me one thing."

We looked at him without saying anything. He had a look of seriousness on his face.

"Promise me," he said, "that you will destroy the photron laser guns when you are finished. They are very dangerous, and earth is not meant to have such a dangerous weapon."

He was right, of course. There was no telling what might happen if these laser guns fell into the wrong hands. Someone might try and use them to take over the whole world!

"I promise we'll get rid of them," I answered.

"Good. Now go. I'll be fine. You two have work to do."

Once again the door of the spaceship chugged open and steps appeared, leading to the ground a few feet below.

"Good-bye," I said, climbing out of the craft.

"Thank you for everything," Brothron said, waving with his hand.

As soon as we stepped out of the craft, the stairs drew back inside. The door groaned shut. The engines roared to life once again, and the ship rose high into the sky. It kept going up, faster and faster, until we couldn't see it anymore.

Brothron was gone, but there was still a Globbling in Alpena.

There was no time to lose.

31

"Come on," I urged Meghan. "We have to find that last Globbling."

We trudged through the field and followed a winding trail that led back to the outskirts of town. The afternoon was wearing on . . . I don't have a watch, but I was sure that it had to be close to six o'clock. I'd have to be home soon for dinner.

But, then again, I wasn't all too worried about dinner anymore. There were a few things a bit more important than eating right now!

"Where do you think he could be?" Meghan asked as we emerged from the forest. A field lay in front of us, and a few houses. I shook my head.

"I have no clue," I answered her. "They eat anything."

"Let's just hope it hasn't eaten any people," she said.

We walked between houses, through a few yards, and came out on US-23 again. We walked along the shoulder of the road, then on the sidewalk. Soon we were downtown.

But so far, there was no sign of the Globbling.

We looked everywhere—and I mean *everywhere!* We went back down to Bay View park, and over to Thunder Bay Shores marina. We walked through parking lots and even a couple of alleys.

But there was no sign of the Globbling.

"Hey Mark!" someone shouted. Meghan and I turned. It was Brad Weller, a friend from school. Actually, nobody calls him Brad. Everybody calls him 'Skeeter'. He came running up to us.

"Hey, Skeeter," I said.

"Man, you gotta watch out!" he said frantically. "Greg Daniels is out looking for you!" He looked at Meghan. "You too!"

"I kind of figured," I said sheepishly. I knew that Greg was still going to be mad at me for what happened this morning on the bus . . . but now he was probably even madder since Meghan kicked him in the shin!

"Where is he now?" Meghan asked.

"I don't know," Skeeter said, shaking his head. "I saw him a while ago. He was limping. He asked if I had seen you."

"Do us a favor," I asked. "If you see him again, tell him you didn't see us." I was trying to make my life last as long as possible.

I think anybody would want to!

"Sure," Skeeter agreed. "But I would keep an eye out for him, if I were you. He's *really* mad at you." He waved good-bye and walked off.

"So, we have two things to worry about," I said to Meghan. "A Globbling . . . and Greg Daniels."

"I think the Globbling is our first concern,"

Meghan replied.

She was right. If I got beat up by Greg Daniels, it sure would hurt. But everyone would go on living. Alpena, and everyone in the city, would be fine.

On the other hand, if that Globbling began eating people, there might be no stopping him. Brothron said that the more a Globbling ate, the bigger it got.

I couldn't think of anything worse than a giant, fat, man-eating Globbling that ate everything in site!

But where would we begin to look? The longer it took us to find the Globbling, the better chance it would have to eat people. We had no clue where to begin.

Suddenly, a shrill scream echoed over the street! It was a woman's scream, and by the way it sounded, she was in trouble!

Oh no!

Were we too late?!?!?

32

"Come on!" I shouted.

We sprang. The screaming was coming from Culligan Plaza. It sounded like maybe the woman was in the parking lot.

Meghan and I ran as fast as we could, sprinting in front of the Royal Knight Cinema. My hand was gripped firmly on the handle of the photron laser gun. I was ready to pull it out at any moment.

We could still hear the woman shrieking in horror. What was happening? Was she being eaten?!?! That would be horrible!

We bolted across the parking lot, ready for

action, ready for anything.

There she was! The woman was standing by her car. The door was open, and she had one hand near her mouth, and one extended out, pointing to something in the car.

We ran up to her.

"What?!?!" I cried. "What's wrong?!?!"

She turned to look at us. "Oh my gosh!" she said. "It's horrible! It's just . . . *horrible!*"

I looked to where she was pointing.

On the seat of her car was a spider. It wasn't even a very big spider, maybe about the size of a quarter.

This is what caused her to scream like that? A spider? I mean . . . it had sounded like she was being eaten alive.

"Oh, it's just a spider," I said, and I reached forward and simply brushed it off the seat with my hand. The spider tumbled to the blacktop and scurried away.

"Thank you," the woman said. "I opened up the car door, and there he was. It was just awful."

Meghan rolled her eyes.

"Well, you're fine now," I said.

"Thank you again," the woman said. She took a good look around the inside of her car to make sure there were no more spiders, then got in.

"What a scaredy-cat," Meghan said quietly.

"Yeah," I said, shaking my head as the woman drove off. "Some people are afraid of everything."

Then I felt a little embarrassed. After all, I was afraid of Greg Daniels. I couldn't even *think* about standing up to him. I guessed I would always be afraid of him.

Like right now.

"Well, well, well," a voice said from behind us.

Meghan and I turned, but I already knew who it was.

Greg Daniels had found us. He was standing in front of the cinema, leaning against a car.

But there was something worse.

It was the Globbling! It was standing a few feet behind Greg, its arms up, ready to pounce on him!

165

33

It was obvious that Greg didn't see the horrible space alien. If he *had*, he probably would be running for his life. Instead, he stepped away from the car and began slowly walking toward us.

"How about that?" he sneered. "Two chickens, pecking around in the parking lot." He laughed.

Behind him the Globbling began to creep forward. It was ugly! It was big and red and gooey-looking, and it was twice the size of an adult.

"Greg," I said. "Don't move. Stay right

where you are." I reached for the photron laser gun.

"Yeah, right," he said. Then, as he spotted the guns, he started laughing. "And just what do you think you're going to do with *those?*" he chuckled. "A couple of water guns?!?! Hah!"

"Greg, there's a space alien right behind you. He's going to attack!"

Greg stopped. His jaw dropped and he covered his mouth with his hands.

"Oh my goodness!" he exclaimed. "I'm going to be eaten by an alien from outer space! Save me, chicken, save me!!"

He was making fun of me!

"Greg, I'm not making this up." I held out the photron laser pistol, aiming at the Globbling.

But Greg was in the way! There was a chance that I might hit Greg with the laser.

"I'm warning you, Greg," I said. "You're in a lot of danger. Right behind you."

"Sure," he said, his voice filling with anger. "You want me to turn so you can get a head start running. Well, I don't think so. I'm going to pound you, chicken." He glanced at Meghan.

"You too, you little weasel. I'm going to—"

I didn't let him finish. The awful Globbling made a sudden rush, and attacked.

I had no choice. I had to shoot. I had to shoot and just hope that the laser missed Greg and hit the Globbling.

A blast of light rocketed out of the barrel of the gun. Greg's eyes grew huge as the beam shot over his shoulder.

Suddenly, there was a thundering blast.

A hit! The Globbling exploded!

Not only did he explode, but tons of red goo went everywhere . . . covering Greg Daniels! He was covered from head to toe in syrup-like red goo! It looked like someone had dumped a truckload of strawberry jelly all over him!

He had a confused look on his face. I was sure that no matter what happened now, Greg Daniels was going to pound me into the ground.

But a strange thing happened. He found it really hard to move!

'Hey . . . what's . . . what's going on?!?!?" he said angrily, trying to move his arms.

It was the goo! It stuck to him like glue, and

169

it made it almost impossible for him to move a muscle!

"Sorry about that," I said.

"No he isn't," Meghan chimed in, smiling from ear to ear.

"What is this stuff?!?!?" Greg demanded. "What did you do to me?!?!"

We started to walk away. Greg posed no threat to us anymore. He certainly couldn't chase us with all of that sticky goo all over his body!

"See ya," I shouted to him. Then I stopped and looked back at him. He was struggling to move.

"Oh, and Greg?" I said.

He slowly looked at me. His nose, his mouth, his eyes . . . his whole face was covered in Globbling goo!

"There's a lot more where that came from," I said, waving the photron laser. "From now on, if you don't leave me alone, I'll just have to use my goo-gun on you."

"*Goo-gun?!?!*" Meghan whispered to me.

"*Shhh,*" I whispered back. "*He doesn't know*

what this is. He probably thinks the gun shot goo all over him."

We walked away, leaving Greg Daniels grunting and groaning, struggling to move his arms and legs.

Hah! Sweet revenge.

34

We walked back through town toward Meghan's house, both of us feeling a lot better. A lot had happened within the past few hours.

"We have to get rid of these photron lasers," I said. "We promised Brothron."

"But how?" Meghan asked. "We have to make sure that no one ever finds them."

We kept walking, wondering how we could get rid of the photron laser pistols. We could bury them, but there still would be a chance that someone could find them. We could try and take them apart, but that might be too dangerous.

"I've got it!" Meghan suddenly cried, snapping her fingers. "There's an old well near our house! It's all dried up, but it's very deep! They're going to bulldoze it over and start to build a house there next week. We could throw them in there!"

That was it!

"Great idea!" I said. "Nobody will ever find them there. Especially if we throw them down the well . . . and it gets filled with dirt!"

We took off running. The well wasn't very far from Meghan's house, and in a few minutes we were there. The well was made of stone, and there was an old wooden roof above it. It looked like it had been there for years.

I drew the photron laser gun from my pocket and took one last look at it.

"You know," I said to Meghan. "This is the only real proof that we have. These laser guns are proof that space aliens came to Alpena."

"Even if we had these, no one will believe what just happened here today. No way."

Meghan was right. What had happened right here in Alpena had been too weird. Even

I wasn't sure I believed what had happened . . . and I had been a part of it!

Reluctantly, I held the photron laser over the well. Meghan did, too.

I let go, and instantly the gun fell away, tumbling into darkness. It disappeared. A couple seconds later, I heard a dull thud as the gun struck the bottom of the dry well.

Meghan let go of her gun, and it fell. There was a thud and a clunk as it struck the other gun.

The two weapons were gone.

"I've got to get home," I said, looking up at the sky. The sun was already beginning to set.

"Me too," Meghan answered. "See you tomorrow at school?"

"Yeah, if I don't get creamed on the bus by Greg Daniels." Meghan laughed, and so did I. It was really funny seeing Greg stuck in all that red goo. I guess if I got beat up now, it wouldn't really matter. Seeing Greg go through the agony of trying to move while covered in Globbling jelly would be worth getting beat up over.

When I got home, did I ever hear it from Mom and Dad! They were *more* than just mad. I had missed dinner, and they had called all of my friends looking for me. I guess it wasn't very smart not to at least check in or something. I thought I was going to get grounded for life. Instead it was a week. That was bad enough.

But it wasn't as bad as things would have been if we hadn't been able to destroy the Globblings!

On the bus the next morning, I waited impatiently for the bus to stop and pick up Greg Daniels. I just knew that he was going to pound me into the ground. I was sure all the kids would be talking about Greg Daniels and me, and how I had ran from him yesterday.

But they weren't. They were all talking about the strange object that had been sighted in the sky over Alpena!

Lots of the kids had seen it. A silver, oblong ball that sped through the sky. Jessica Moore even swore she saw it go into the water.

Hah! If they only knew the truth!

Finally the bus stopped in front of Greg's house. He got on. He took one look at me, and quickly looked away. Then he found the seat farthest from me, and sat down.

Strange!

But even stranger yet, when the bus stopped, Greg waited in his seat! He was the *last* one off! It really seemed like he was trying to avoid me! Maybe he believed that remark I made about the 'goo-gun' after all.

When I got to school, Meghan was waiting for me by my locker.

"I got grounded," she said, frowning.

"Me too," I said. "Did you hear anyone talking about the UFO over Alpena last night?"

Meghan smiled. "Yeah," she said, with a smirk. "Only *we* know different."

The bell rang. "See you sixth hour," Meghan said.

"See ya," I replied, and went to my first class.

As you can imagine, what most kids wanted to talk about was the UFO. I didn't say anything. What could I say? But it was kind of fun, listening to everyone's ideas of what they *thought* they saw.

There was a new girl in class that sat behind me. I've only spoken with her a couple times. She said that she and her family had just moved to Alpena from a city called Gaylord.

She didn't say anything about the UFO's either. Rather, she seemed happy just to listen to everyone else, just like I was.

While the class was in a heated discussion about whether or not there's life on other planets, I felt her lean forward.

"You know," she whispered. *"All this stuff about UFO's is pretty strange. But it's nothing like what happened to me and my friends in Gaylord last summer."*

"Like what?" I asked.

"Gargoyles," she whispered. *"Real gargoyles."*

Huh? Was she saying that there were real live gargoyles . . . in *Gaylord?*

"They were everywhere," she continued. "They—"

She was interrupted by the school bell.

178

Class was over. We both stood up, and I spoke.

"Real gargoyles? Are you sure?"

She nodded, then glanced around to make sure no one else was listening. "Meet me in the cafeteria during lunch and I'll tell you all about it."

Gargoyles? In Gaylord!?!?!

Wow!

Next in the 'Michigan Chillers'
series . . . .
#5 : 'Gargoyles of Gaylord!'
Go to the next page for a few
chilling chapters!

The first thing you need to know about me is that I am afraid of the dark. Dark rooms, dark hallways, dark stairs . . . I'm just afraid of the dark, period.

I think a lot of people are afraid of the dark, but they just don't admit it.

But I have a reason to be afraid! You would have a reason, too, if you knew what I went through last summer.

My name is Corrine. Corrine MacArthur. But everybody calls me Corky. In fact, not many people even know my real name.

Everybody—even my school teachers—call me Corky. Actually, I kind of like the nickname.

Corky.

I haven't always been afraid of the dark. Up until last summer, I don't think I was afraid of the dark at all.

But something happened last summer that changed all that.

It was the middle of June, and school had just got out. It was the beginning of summer. I love summer! The days are longer and warmer, and there's so much to do. We live in Gaylord, which is a small city in the middle of northern lower Michigan. It's pretty cool.

In the summertime, we get to stay out late. Well, later than we get to stay out during the school year, anyway. All of my friends on the block get together and play yard games like 'kick the can' and 'ghost in the graveyard.' We play till long after dark.

On this particular night, there was about ten of us playing outside. It had just gotten dark, and the streetlight was on. We had just finished playing a game, and my friend Ashley and I were sitting on the curb, watching giant June bugs swarm around the street light. June bugs are noisy . . . they sound like little airplanes flying through the sky. Their wings clap like playing cards clipped between bicycle spokes.

"Well, I'd better get home," Ashley said. "I'm supposed to be home by ten."

"See ya later," I said, standing up. A lock of my black hair fell in front of my face, and I brushed it away. I started walking across our yard, then I stopped and turned back around. "You want to go to the park with us tomorrow?" I asked Ashley. We don't live too far from the park. There's a creek there, and a big field. I like to wade in the creek and catch crayfish. Ashley thinks they're gross. But we always have a lot of fun.

She stopped and turned.

"Yeah, sure," she replied. "See you at the park in the morning." And with that, she turned and began walking home. She lives only a few houses down from us.

The night was unusually dark. There was no moon, and the day had been cloudy. The sky

185

above had no stars. But the street light lit up everything in the yard.

I was almost to our porch when all of a sudden, everything went black!

The lights . . . all of them . . . went out! The street lights, the porch light, all of the lights in our house . . . even the lights in the other houses on the street . . . went out!

I was in total darkness!

Now remember . . . at this time, I wasn't afraid of the dark. It sure was strange that all of the lights went off like that. But it's happened before. In Gaylord, we can get some pretty fierce snowstorms in the winter. Once in a while, the power will go out. It's kind of fun, really. Dad will light a fire in the fireplace, and sometimes we even cook hot dogs and marshmallows. It makes me wish we had snowstorms more often.

But this was the middle of summer. It was strange that the power just went off like that.

And it was *dark!* It was darker than I had ever seen before. I couldn't see the porch ten feet in front of me. I couldn't see any trees. I couldn't see *anything*.

I stopped dead in my tracks. I didn't want to accidentally smack into the porch or into a tree.

I turned, looking down the street . . . or, where I *thought* the street should be. It was far too dark to see the street or any street signs.

I wondered what caused all of the lights to go off. Maybe there was a problem at the power plant. Maybe the whole city was out of power!

All of a sudden, I heard Ashley's voice calling out.

"Corky?!?!" she shouted. "Are you still outside?!?!?" Her voice echoed down the street.

"Yes!" I shouted back.

"It sure is dark!" she hollered.

"Like 'duh'!" I replied loudly. "It's a power failure. I don't see any lights on anywhere."

"I can't even see my own house!" she shouted.

"Me neither!" I shouted back. "And I'm

only ten feet away from it!"

"Too bad it isn't Halloween," she laughed. Ashley has this really funny giggle, and it sounded even funnier, echoing down the street. It was like there were two or three Ashley's laughing. It sure was strange, standing here in the dark and talking to her without being able to see her.

"Well, I'm going to try and make it to my house," she said. "But it's so dark, I can't even see my nose!"

"Be careful of Mr. Hansel's house," I said loudly. "I hear that he eats kids!"

"Knock it off!" she shouted back to me. "That's just a story!"

Mr. Hansel is a strange man that lives in the house next to Ashley's. We hardly ever see him, and he only leaves his house at night. Someone made up a story that he eats children, but I've never believed it.

What's even weirder is that Mr. Hansel has a fenced in back yard. But it's not just a fence . . . it's a wooden fence. It's almost eight feet tall, and you can't even see through it.

There's no telling what he has in his back yard. Some people say that there's an old graveyard back there. Other people say that they hear strange noises coming from behind the fence, but they don't know what they are. One of my friends at school swears that he saw Mr. Hansel actually climb over the fence! That would be almost impossible! I mean . . . Mr. Hansel is old . . . and the fence is taller than he is!

There are other stories, too. Some people say that Mr. Hansel is a troll that can turn into any kind of animal that he wants.

But those are just stories. Nobody can do stuff like that. When I was little, I used to believe the stories. I thought that they were real.

I've only seen Mr. Hansel a few times. He's got messy gray hair, and he stoops forward when he walks. And he's always got a mean look on his face.

At least, whenever I've seen him, he's got a mean look on his face! Mr. Hansel doesn't look like a nice man. In fact, he looks scary. Scary and mean.

"I'll see you later," Ashley shouted one final

time from a few houses down.

"Later," I shouted back, and I carefully began walking through the darkness to the porch.

In the next instant, a shrill scream pierced the dark night! It was a long, painful wail that echoed up and down the street!

Ashley!

3

Ashley's scream rang down the block, echoing like the Grand Canyon.

"Ashley!" I screamed. *"What's wrong?!?"*

But she didn't answer me. She just screamed and screamed and screamed.

Suddenly, her screaming stopped. Her voice was cut short, like there was someone . . . or something . . . that had stopped her.

What could I do? It was too dark to see anything.

But I had to help Ashley. Something had happened, and I was sure that she needed help.

"Ashley?" I called out, taking a few brave steps in her direction. I strained my eyes to see her, but it was no use. It was just too dark.

"Ashley?" I called out again.

No answer. What had happened to her?

I began walking faster, hoping that I wouldn't trip or smack into something in the dark.

I walked across our driveway, and then felt my sneakers sink back into the squishy grass. I took a few steps, then stopped.

I could hear moaning coming from the next yard. It was muffled and soft, and it was hard to hear, but I knew who it was.

Ashley.

She was hurt!

Without thinking, I took off running blindly through the dark.

"Ashley!" I shouted. "Where are you?!? Where are you?!?!"

More moaning.

I took off running again, but I didn't get far. I had only taken about four steps when my foot caught on something and I stumbled, falling forward. I raised my hands out in front of me as I fell, and I hit the ground with a heavy thud.

"Oooof!" I said, as the wind was knocked out of me.

"Ouch!" Ashley groaned.

I had tripped over her!

"Are you okay?" I said, getting to my knees.

"Yeah, I think so," she said. Her voice was tight and I could tell she was hurting. "But it didn't help when you ran into me."

"Well, how was I supposed to know that you were laying on the grass?" I snapped. "It's so dark, I can't see a thing."

All of a sudden a loud 'pop!' filled the air, and all of the lights came back on! The streetlight in front of our house shined brightly in the night, and windows from houses glowed a creamy yellow.

And for the first time, I realized we were in Mr. Hansel's yard.

I stood up and walked over to Ashley.

There was blood on her leg! Just above her knee, she had a nasty scrape.

"Yuuuuck," I said. "Does it hurt bad?"

"It did for a minute," she answered. "For a minute, it really hurt bad."

"Hold on a second," I said, peering at the wound on her leg. "Look. It almost looks like you've been bitten by something."

Ashley kneeled forward, looking at the scrape on her leg. There were two deep gashes—bite marks—that had punctured the skin.

"That's gross," she said. "It's gross and it hurts."

"What did you scrape it on?" I asked.

"That," Ashley pointed. "Right there."

I turned and looked at the shadowy form she was pointing to. I hadn't seen it earlier. Actually, I didn't remember ever seeing it there before. In fact, I was *certain* that I hadn't seen it before.

I walked closer to the object. It was about half my height, and about as big around as a beach ball.

What in the world, I thought.

But when I got closer, I knew what it was.

A gargoyle.

I drew a sudden, quick breath, and covered my mouth with my hand.

A gargoyle.

Not a real gargoyle, of course . . . but one of those stone ones that you see in gardens. They're just statues, but some of them sure look real.

And this one looked *very* real, that's for sure.

It was all gray, made out of cement. It had a fat face with a pudgy nose. Sharp, piercing eyes glared back at me. In its mouth were four angry fangs . . . two on the top and two on the bottom. Two thick wings grew from its back. The gargoyle was in a hunched position, as if it was about to fly.

"What is it?" Ashley asked, finally getting to her feet. She held one hand near her wound as she limped toward me.

"A cement gargoyle," I replied, still staring at the statue. I knew it wasn't real, but it just looked so weird. It looked so real, even though it was only made out of cement. I kept staring at it. I had never seen it in the yard before.

"Eeeeww, that's gross," Ashley said as she stopped at my side. "What would Mr. Hansel be doing with a gargoyle in his yard?"

"Who knows?" I replied. "Nothing that Mr. Hansel does makes any sense, anyway."

I couldn't stop staring at the statue. Something in its mouth caught my attention. Suddenly, I knew what it was.

"Ashley . . . look at that," I said quietly. "Look in its mouth."

Ashley leaned closer. "What?" she asked.

"Look in its mouth," I repeated. "Look at its teeth!"

She bent closer.

"That's even MORE gross!" she said loudly, shivering.

On one of the teeth, a tiny blood stain remained.

Ashley's blood.

"That must be where I ran into him," Ashley said, glancing down at the wound on her leg.

"Yeah," I replied. "Either that . . . or he BIT YOU!!!" As I said the words *'bit you'*, I suddenly grabbed Ashley with both hands around her waist. She shrieked and doubled over. We both laughed and laughed.

"I gotta go," she finally said. She bent her head down, inspecting the wound on her leg. "I've got to get this cleaned before it gets infected."

"And before you get bit again," I laughed. Ashley laughed, too. "See you tomorrow," I said, and I watched her as she walked across the darkened yard toward her house. When I saw her shadow reach her porch, I hollered out.

"Bye!" I shouted.

"See you tomorrow!" she said. I heard the

front door of her house open, and light streamed out. The door closed with a thud.

The night was quiet. Singing crickets filled the air, and the sound of cars traveling on nearby Otsego street were the only things I could hear.

And so, as I stood in the dim light of the street lamp, the sound of fluttering wings close by caused me to nearly jump out of my skin.

I spun, and what I saw almost made me faint.

The cement gargoyle that had been sitting in the yard had taken flight!

It was enormous! Its wings beat the air like a giant owl, and it spun through the air with the speed of a bat!

I couldn't believe what I was seeing. The gargoyle swung out of sight in the shadows, then suddenly came back into view as it dipped beneath the street light in front of our house. Then it wheeled back around, its wings outstretched, swooping through the sky. I could only see its shadow, but I didn't need to see any more. It was flying faster, zipping through the night sky like a mad hornet. I could hear its wings pounding the air like a drum.

Wha-whoosh . . . wha-whoosh . . . .

Closer . . . .

Wha-whoosh . . . wha-whoosh . . . .

Closer . . . .

Wha-whoosh . . . wha-whoosh . . . .

Closer still!

Oh no! It was coming for me!

About the author

Johnathan Rand is the author of the best-selling **'Chillers'** series, now with over 2,000,000 copies in print. In addition to the **'Chillers'** series, Rand is also the author of the **'Adventure Club'** series, including **'Ghost in the Graveyard'**, **'Ghost in the Grand'**, and **'The Haunted Schoolhouse'**, three collections of thrilling, original short stories. When Mr. Rand and his wife are not traveling to schools and book signings, they live in a small town in northern lower Michigan with their two dogs, Abby and Lily Munster. He is currently working on more 'Chillers', as well as a new series for younger readers entitled **'Freddie Fernortner, Fearless First Grader'**. His popular website features hundreds of photographs, stories, and art work. Visit:

www.americanchillers.com

Also by Johnathan Rand:

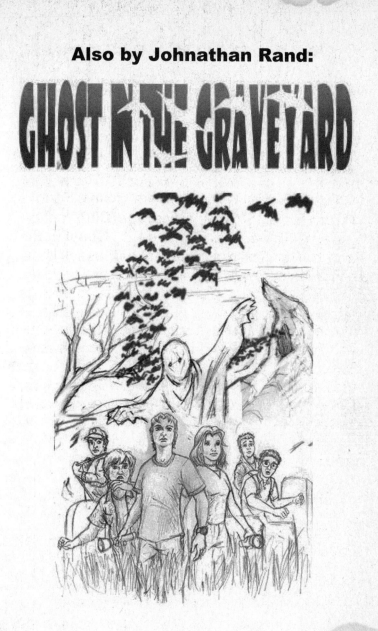

ALIENS ATTACK ALPENA WORD SEARCH!

```
W U H U O E F N W Z Z G H J V N J T Y K
W E C H Y A E X N U K P S S B L G E S Y
E T Q W O U N K P A H E B D A B R E N G
Z C E V Q G J D M O K R V K J X F R A L
P N U I V C X O T A L I E N S D R T Y E
S N O R H T O R B Z P H I E Q Q H S A O
T K P F H G O O K M U A I E Q U V M Y R
M E G H A N A N D R E W S L N S P L J F
A C F V L I G H O Y F L R D G K I O N U
I P X A S L H N V L E F E Z C M H S F B
V S S J O B Z O R I E R L U J N S I C C
T E Y B G B O T N U B N L E A H E H K N
R T B S G O O A T A B L I T V K C C R E
H L P K K L D Q Y B I K H C F N A P A P
A T R X A G H S N G A A C N A Y P V P K
R A F G E A H N A Y N Z N A K K S W W S
U L Q R E O R N E R E C A D L O F O E R
D N G D R X P O A S P U G N L B O K I O
Q M T E L L I N A R L C I O P Y K A V E
V Y S R A V D A S Z A T H G G I K R Y T
B T U Z L U G X R H W C C R O G F O A E
K C A T T A I Z B E W N I A L O O T B M
W O X F K J I M J T N A M V S K M N Y D
Q C C A D H J T O Z T O I L R H C N N W
```

Alpena	Thunder Bay Shores
Bay View Park	Photron Laser
Globbla	Globbling
Mark Blackburn	Johnathan Rand
Meghan Andrews	Michigan Chillers
Aliens	Attack
Meteor	Vargondan
Brothron	Greg Daniels
Lake Huron	Culligan Plaza
Spaceship	Chisolm Street

WORD SCRAMBLE!

Unscramble the words and place the new words in the blanks!

ohrnrtbo	_ _ _ _ _ _ _ _
eggr iasneld	_ _ _ _ _ _ _ _ _ _ _
oeetrm	_ _ _ _ _ _
aelrs	_ _ _ _ _
nradnvago	_ _ _ _ _ _ _ _ _
yba evwi akrp	_ _ _ _ _ _ _ _ _ _
rkma aknclrubb	_ _ _ _ _ _ _ _ _ _ _ _
pcapssieh	_ _ _ _ _ _ _ _ _
nehgma asdernw	_ _ _ _ _ _ _ _ _ _ _ _ _
pnaeal	_ _ _ _ _ _
lneia	_ _ _ _ _
klea nuorh	_ _ _ _ _ _ _ _ _
gbinsolblg	_ _ _ _ _ _ _ _ _ _
mgnihica lihercls	_ _ _ _ _ _ _ _ _ _ _ _ _ _ _

Join the official

AMERICAN CHILLERS

FAN CLUB!

Visit www.americanchillers.com for details

All AudioCraft books are proudly printed, bound, and manufactured in the United States of America, utilizing American resources, labor, and materials.

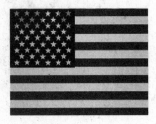

USA